Sacred Bird

NAATOYIPI'KSSI

Pearl Long Time Squirrel

COVER ILLUSTRATION BY BARBARA COTTON

◆ FriesenPress

One Printers Way
Altona, MB R0G 0B0
Canada

www.friesenpress.com

Original Cover Design and Illustration by Barbara Cotton

Author Photo by Alexis Long Time Squirrel

ISBN
978-1-03-918270-7 (Hardcover)
978-1-03-918269-1 (Paperback)
978-1-03-918271-4 (eBook)

1. FICTION, INDIGENOUS

Distributed to the trade by The Ingram Book Company

The book is dedicated to

Carrie Hunt

for sharing and encouraging me
to write the story.

SACRED BIRD

(Naatoyipi'kssi)

CHAPTER 1

REMEMBERING

That spring day of long ago, before this area was populated, Sacred Bird and her people had just moved to their summer camp. Their days were filled with chores that needed to get done for survival. That day promised to be a beautiful day.

Sacred Bird stepped out of the tepee and took a deep breath of fresh air as she stretched and yawned as if to chase the sleep away and greet the new day. The morning air was crisp and clear. She enjoyed a beautiful day and this morning promised to be just that. The birds were singing as if they were competing to see which one could sing the loudest and which one could sing the best song. The people were stirring and already the young men were getting ready to leave, eager to prove their hunting skills. The women were busy getting ready for a full day of work. The children were out and about, playing and laughing, and somewhere in one of the tepees a child was crying. Even the dogs were milling about as if to get ready to pounce on any scrap of food that may be thrown their way.

Oh, how this morning reminded Sacred Bird of a morning a long time ago, a generation ago. She stood for a moment to remember. She remembered the details of that morning as if it was yesterday. She had mixed emotions about the outcome of that traumatic event. She silently thanked the Creator. Creator had been with her and had watched over her family. Deep down, she had a feeling of emptiness for her daughter. This is an emptiness she will not forget as long as she lives.

She remembered that morning. She had gotten up early to take care of the morning meal for her husband before he left with the hunting party. She had fed the old people and the children before she got ready to tackle her chores.

She had taken the water containers to fetch the water from the river and she had also taken the rawhide rope to tie the firewood she was going to gather from the woods at the same time. She usually did the chores separately, but that morning she had decided to gather firewood at the same time. That was a decision she would later regret.

In those days, the women had so many chores to do before each day ended. Every chore was backbreaking, but they managed. Sometimes they got together to help each other out, but that morning, Sacred Bird had decided to do the easy chores first before asking for help.

Her husband's elderly parents were just finishing their morning prayers. She was tidying up, putting away the food that was left over from breakfast before gathering the water containers and rope. She decided to ask her two-year-old daughter, Sacred Feather Woman, to come with her. This would give the elders a little time to relax before the day got too hectic. Even though her children are eager to spend the day with their grandparents, the short time they will spend away from their grandparents allowed each to play on their own.

Sacred Bird always enjoyed spending time with her daughter. The time away from her grandparents allowed Sacred Feather Woman to see the birds and small animals that usually scurried away when people were on the path . . . her daughter liked animals, especially little baby ones. Sacred Feather Woman was always pleasant, always inquisitive, and always ready to help whenever she could. Sacred Bird's two sons had not wasted any time; they had left and gone with the other boys before Sacred Bird and Sacred Feather Woman even set their feet outside. Once outside, Sacred Feather Woman paused to let her eyes adjust to the sun's brightness. Sacred Bird took her daughter's tiny hand and led her down the path toward the river.

'It is going to be a beautiful day' . . . she thought to herself, 'the birds are singing.' The breeze was playfully rustling the leaves, and she heard an eagle somewhere in the sky above. She looked up at the sky. There were tiny wisps of clouds floating lazily eastward across the sky. She took a deep breath of the fresh spring air.

Her daughter tugged at her hand and brought her back to reality. Sacred Feather Woman was eager to join the group of women and children ahead of them. The tug and the sounds of happy voices brought Sacred Bird back to the matter of the chores. She shook her head as if to shake the daydreaming off. She was a little surprised at herself, she was not usually this attentive to her surroundings . . . oh, well, she thought to herself, 'I should take a little time to notice the new plants, the blue sky, the majestic mountains, the fresh air, and be thankful to the Creator for providing a beautiful place for the people.'

As they rounded a bend, they met some of the women returning to the camp, they smiled and greeted each other. Their arms were laden with water containers and their children noisily followed. A few children hung back to explore and inspect the plants and insects by the path. Each one found something to take with them back to the camp as a keepsake or as a plaything.

Another slight bend and the river came into view. At the river's edge, a few women were conversing and laughing, their children wading in the water downstream. Everyone was so happy.

There was a clearing just before the 'beach' area and there were tall bushes on either side of the clearing. The river's edge was sandy, with a few big rocks in the water serving as stepping-stones for the women while they filled their water skins. She paused and exchanged a few pleasantries with the women and agreed to visit with them later in the day after most of her chores were done. Most of these women were relations either by birth or by marriage.

Sacred Bird started to sink back into her thoughts about spring . . . 'Spring is a happy time of the year, and every living thing becomes new. Spring is the time of the year the plants seem happy to compete for attention. They display the colours of their new leaves and petals, and send forth the aromas and fragrances, which are not easily ignored. Spring is when every plant becomes new again. Spring is when the animals give birth'.

She looked around and saw that her daughter had taken her moccasins off and was wading in the river's edge not far from her. A few of the women were looking closely at the bushes, inspecting and admiring the flowers which would turn into berries very soon. Sacred Bird carefully stepped on a large rock and squatted down to fill the water containers. While the water containers were filling, she looked around and noticed just a few steps away . . . the tiny fish playfully darting in and out of the crevices of the rocks.

Other women and children were getting ready to return to the camp. Sacred Bird's elderly neighbour, Last Woman, called out to her . . . "Hurry, Sacred Bird, hurry and get your water, everyone is going back . . ."

Sacred Bird yelled for her to start already and told her, "I should not be too long."

As she started the second container, Sacred Bird noticed that the voices of the other women and children were quickly fading. She plunged the container more into the water to coax it to fill up quickly. After it was filled, she hurried as fast as she could, tying the containers closed so the water would not spill. Sacred Feather Woman was still standing in the water. Sacred Bird called her daughter.

Sacred Feather Woman did not answer right away, instead she reached down to pick up a small rock from the water. Sacred Bird called her again, a little impatiently, and Sacred Feather Woman carefully stepped out of the water and started to walk toward her mother. Her little hands glistening in the sunlight and clutching the rock.

Her eyes fixed on the rock, she walked toward her mother. "Na'aa, look at this pretty rock," she said as she held out the small red shiny rock.

Sacred Bird took the rock, examined it, and at the same time said, "Yes, it is a pretty rock, but hurry, we must catch up with the rest . . . It is not safe to be by ourselves . . . here, I'll get your moccasins and place them over your shoulder for now and we will put them on your feet at the edge of the woods, ok?"

Sacred Bird took her daughter's moccasins and tied them together and placed them over Sacred Feather Woman's shoulder, allowing her to walk barefoot on the sandy beach and the well-worn path. Then she took her hand and steered her daughter down the path as she stooped to pick up the containers of water and swung the rope over her shoulders.

With a little coaxing and gentle pushing, her daughter slowly started walking ahead of her. As they walked, Sacred Bird would reach down to pick up a few pieces of dried wood which were on the side of the path and place them under her arms. While reaching down to pick up another piece of wood, she noticed some more dried branches, which were longer, just a few steps away in the woods. She decided it would not take up too much time to take them. She called Sacred Feather Woman to stop and wait for her. She carefully placed the water containers on the side of the path and beside the water containers; she laid out the rawhide rope and placed the few dried branches on it.

She stepped into the woods, taking care not to get scratched by the overhanging branches and dried twigs and telling Sacred Feather Woman, "Don't follow me, wait right there. I am just going to get those long pieces of wood. I won't take long."

Sacred Feather Woman did not answer, she just nodded. Sacred Feather Woman was still fascinated with the rock.

As Sacred Bird turned, she suddenly had an eerie feeling of someone watching her. The bright and peaceful morning took on a foreboding air of impending danger. She tried to convince herself that it was because they were alone and away from the safety of the others and the camp. Sacred Bird shrugged the feeling off and decided to venture on and take those dried branches and be on their way.

She could not shake that eerie feeling. She felt as if a pair of eyes or more were fixed on her. That eerie feeling made her feel uneasy. Shivers went down her spine and she tried to shake them off by shaking her shoulders. She stood still and looked around, but the bushes were too thick to see anything. She stood for a moment straining her ears to hear something. She heard the river's rippling sounds as it raced over the rocks, she heard the birds singing in the distance, and she heard dogs barking in the camp. Somewhere in the bushes behind her, she heard the crackling of dried leaves and the breaking of dried twigs as if someone or something was stepping on them. She tried to reassure herself that it must be a small animal in the bushes.

Sacred Bird turned and started to reach for the dried branch in front of her when out of nowhere came the rushing sounds of hooves, of snorts, and of the bushes being pushed apart. Then she saw them.

There was no time to run or hide or even to get to Sacred Feather Woman to protect her. She froze in her tracks, she could not move or utter any words, she could not tell Sacred Feather Woman to run to the camp as fast as she could.

Sacred Bird's heart started to beat fast. She felt weak with fear and then she panicked. Just as she turned to run toward Sacred Feather Woman, she saw the horsemen. One came straight at her. The man on horseback got to where she was standing so quickly she did not have time to move. He reached down and grabbed her. She lost her balance but did not fall. The man struggled to get Sacred Bird to sit on the horse. In all the confusion, Sacred Bird could only think of freeing herself. She started to fight; kicking, punching, and screaming. Trying with all her might to free herself from his grip, they almost fell off the horse. To stop Sacred Bird from struggling, the man started to hit her while holding onto her.

He almost succeeded in knocking her unconscious, but Sacred Bird eased her struggle. She had to find out where her baby was. Did they leave her? Or did they take her also? She thought of what her daughter might be going through; then she heard her daughter's cries and screams. Sacred Feather Woman was calling out to her mother. Sacred Bird felt pain and agony for her daughter and started calling out to her daughter, hoping her daughter would hear her and be reassured that she was still alive. The man who had grabbed her was frantically trying to keep Sacred Bird from yelling. He started punching and slapping her.

Sacred Bird felt pains shooting through her body and she finally realized that it was useless to fight. Sacred Bird still had enough strength to fight but she had an overwhelming need to protect her daughter. It was clear then that Sacred Bird must do everything possible to stay alive for Sacred Feather Woman's sake. Sacred Bird had to stay strong and alert. She kept telling herself to calm down and remain calm. To struggle more would be a waste of energy, and she must conserve her energy. Sacred Bird must protect her daughter from whatever danger lies ahead.

When she finally calmed herself, she looked around and saw that they had gone quite a distance from where they were picked up. Any amount of screaming was not going to help. Her thoughts turned to Sacred Feather Woman. She hoped they could slow this group enough to allow the men from the home camp to track them and come to their rescue. Sacred Bird knew deep in her heart that it was futile to think they would be rescued because the men from the camp usually return after the sun sets, and it was not even midday yet. The sun was still to the east.

It was then that Sacred Bird realized the man with whom she was riding had not relaxed his grip on her wrist. The grip on her arm made the pain so excruciating that it seemed to pulsate through to her heart. She tried to wrench her wrist away from the grip, but the man only gripped her wrist harder. Her thoughts full of questions, 'when is he going to relax his grip on my wrist and let the blood circulate through to ease the pain?' She was getting a headache and a sore neck from lying face-down across the back of the horse. She tried to spit. The spit in her mouth tasted like blood, but her mouth would not cooperate, her lips and jaw were swollen. Then she realized this man must think she would try to run back if given the chance and wanted to make sure she did not escape. Sacred Bird tried to straighten, but he held her down. She tried to relax but it was impossible.

After what seemed a long time, the man finally got her to sit up straight in front of him. She tried to take a good look at these men who so rudely took her and her daughter. There were four men; two seemed to be older than the other two, although she would guess not much older. The one who picked her up seemed to be a leader, a minor one maybe. He seemed to be giving orders, and the other three men would not hesitate to follow his orders.

Sacred Bird had a sinking feeling. She felt sick to her stomach when she realized that she is a victim of those abductions that she had heard about. She never realized she would ever be in a situation such as this.

She and Sacred Feather Woman have been kidnapped and taken away from the safety and protection of loved ones and the camp. They have been taken away from the place they have been so accustomed to. Their dignity and self-worth have been taken away. Sacred Bird wondered if she and Sacred Feather Woman would ever be able to go home. What is to become of them? Are they now only possessions and will they be treated less than humans?

Her mind raced with thoughts of the unknown. Will they ever see their loved ones? How will they return? Why did these people come and take them? What is the purpose of all this? Sacred Bird did not have the answers and she could not think of any explanations, so she resigned herself and tried to think of a way out of this situation. She could not think clearly.

Sacred Bird looked around for her little Sacred Feather Woman and saw her daughter riding with one of the men behind them. Sacred Feather Woman looked so fragile and helpless. Sacred Bird's heart ached to hold her daughter's tiny body and comfort her and to let her know she would not let any harm come to her. As she looked back at her little girl, the man with her said some words she could not understand and then he grabbed her hair and jerked her head to look to the front. That was the beginning of her journey of suffering.

Sacred Bird did not know what the future had in store for them. If she had known, she would have made every effort to escape before the long journey. How was she to know the pain she would endure, both emotional and physical? Her endurance and stamina would be tested. How could she know that part of her life would be taken away? She could never take the love and security of family for granted. The experience would forever be in her mind.

CHAPTER 2

THE JOURNEY NORTH

The journey was tiring and painful. Sacred Bird was not used to riding. The horses were getting tired too. They had followed the river to the north and what she thought was a full day turned out to be less than a half day's ride. They did not make any stops until they got to a clearing. Sacred Bird felt a little disoriented when she got off the horse, which must have been caused by the shock of the events and from the many blows she received. She was not quite sure which direction the home camp was at first.

Once she was on the ground, she was intent on getting to her little Sacred Feather Woman. She was about to run to her when the man grabbed her arm and held her back. Sacred Bird called out to her daughter, and the man let Sacred Feather Woman come to her. Sacred Bird reached out to her daughter. To her horror, she almost fell over, she could hardly stand up! Sacred Bird was not used to riding horses the way she was forced to ride, her head and legs hanging over the horse's back, and that was only the beginning.

Once her daughter was in her arms, Sacred Bird felt relieved. Sacred Feather Woman was unharmed. Her daughter trembled from the events of the abduction; it took Sacred Bird a while before her daughter finally relaxed. The men were talking in their language, and she could not understand what they were saying. She sat in the shade of a big tree with Sacred Feather Woman in her arms. Her daughter was so exhausted she fell asleep almost immediately. Sacred Bird was so tired. The ride had also made her sleepy, but she could not afford to fall asleep. She sat there and tried to collect her thoughts.

After Sacred Feather Woman fell asleep, Sacred Bird examined her injuries and found that she had received numerous scratches; some were very deep and bleeding, and bruises made her skin very dark. Sacred Bird remembered that she must have received the scratches from the over-hanging branches and dried twigs where she was abducted and the bruises from the blows the man inflicted on her. She felt the stinging pain of the deep scratches that seemed to be all over her body. Her body ached from the bruises and her head throbbed with pain. She examined Sacred Feather Woman, and to her relief her daughter had not received any scratches or injuries, but she had lost her moccasins. She will have to make this journey without moccasins and will have to be very careful to not get any cuts or slivers.

Sacred Bird looked around at her surroundings and saw the 'Big Ridge' southeast of them. She realized that there must be a camp just over the small hill. She immediately planned an escape in her mind. She was convinced she would make it, if she could just get to the horse on the end. She had seen the horses tied to the trees not far from where she was sitting, each horse restrained with a rope tied to another rope, which was tied to two trees to keep them from running off. Mentally picturing the getaway, she tried to figure out whether she should or should not, and then she had doubts . . . even if she tried, she is in no condition to move fast and she would be caught before she had a chance.

What if she could get to the camp and find out there are not enough people to help her? Would she be endangering the lives of other women and children in that camp? What if there are more men with these men? How many more men are there? What if these men are members of a larger war party and the larger party is waiting at a certain point? There were so many questions she needed answered. Sacred Bird decided she would wait for the right time. Her thoughts turned to the camp and wondered when they would miss them and come after them.

Just then she noticed the fifth man tending to the horses that she had not noticed or seen before. 'How long has he been around the horses? Was he there with the horses before we got here? Is he the only one or are there others waiting at a different place? How many men are in this group . . . how many more horses do they have? Where did they get the horses?' Her thoughts were still on these unanswered questions when one of the men came over and handed her a piece of dried meat.

She realized that she had not eaten that morning and was hungry. She ate half of the dried meat and saved the other half for her daughter. She had not thought about food and was thankful for being able to eat despite her swollen mouth and sore jaw. She looked down at Sacred Feather Woman, who slept soundly and looked as if she did not have a care, which made Sacred Bird glad. Sacred Feather Woman is too young and innocent, she should not have to worry. Sacred Feather Woman looked so peaceful.

'Is this a dream? No, it seems more like a nightmare . . . that what was happening to us is not real . . .' Sacred Bird thought to herself.

The man's gruff voice startled her. He reached down, took her arm, and lifted her up. Sacred Bird had a hard time getting up; it seemed as if every part of her body was sore. When the man grabbed Sacred Bird's arm, her arms almost gave out. It took her whole being to try and keep her arms from giving out and dropping Sacred Feather Woman and to not cry out in pain. Sacred Bird stood up and tried to keep her balance. It was then she noticed the horses were fresh. Her heart sank as she realized that this was going to be a tiring journey with noticeably short rests. The men seemed to be prepared. They have more horses, and more horses mean that they will be changing horses often.

Then the one who rode with Sacred Bird's little daughter came and took Sacred Feather Woman, who awoke with a start. Sacred Bird kissed her daughter and quietly told her it was ok and that she would be right there with her, but Sacred Feather Woman had to ride with the man.

Her daughter looked at her with sad eyes. Sacred Bird kissed her again and whispered, "You are going to be safe with him, he will not let you fall off, and I'll be right beside you, ok?" Sacred Feather Woman nodded, her tiny hands still outstretched. Sacred Bird's eyes felt the stinging pain of tears welling up and she tried to prevent them from flooding out.

The day was starting to become hot, and sitting in the shade did not cool her enough to stop her from perspiring. She again started to feel the pains of the scratches, the pain increasing each time the many drops of perspiration eased into the scratches. The cool breeze she had felt earlier had stopped. She dreaded the journey, not for her sake, but for Sacred Feather Woman's. The journey should be tolerable if the travelling was done during the evenings.

The leader said a few words Sacred Bird could not understand and shoved her. Sacred Bird guessed he wanted her to get on the horse, so she started to limp to the horse. He stopped her and pushed her down to sit on the ground. This confused Sacred Bird, but after he took a small rawhide rope from his bag, she realized he was going to tie her. First he tied her wrists together, and then he tied her right wrist to her right ankle. Sacred Bird realized that her chances of escaping were nil and any hopes of being able to slip away in the night had also been significantly brought to a halt. To try would involve more struggling. After the leader finished tying her wrists and ankle, he grabbed her by the arms and almost tossed her onto the horse.

They travelled along the river until they got to a place where the two rivers meet. They crossed the river at a shallow part and stopped long enough to refresh themselves as the men watered the horses. After they stopped, Sacred Bird fell off the horse and landed on some rocks on the shore, further injuring her bruised hip. She managed to hobble around and refresh herself. Little Sacred Feather Woman was very understanding and attempted to help her mother. The leader just shook his head after Sacred Bird motioned him to untie one rope. Sacred Bird could not hold Sacred Feather Woman as she did before her wrists and ankle were tied, but Sacred Feather Woman did not seem to mind. She gave her mother a look that Sacred Bird interpreted to say she understood. Sacred Bird tried to explain to her daughter that the man did not want her to escape.

The men sat by the river and planned whatever they were planning, then after a while they all got up and started preparing for the next part of the journey. Sacred Feather Woman and Sacred Bird sat by the river not far from them. Her daughter was throwing little pebbles into the water while Sacred Bird surveyed her surroundings. She could not see too much but across the river, where they came from. The bushes were thick among the many trees across the river. There did not seem to be anyone around.

Sometimes, in her mind, Sacred Bird hoped above hope to have someone following to rescue them. She started to imagine someone trying to rescue her and her daughter, just following and waiting for the right moment. But she knew there was no one because she had made a point of searching the horizon when they travelled along the top of the hill to make a detour and avoid a cliff on their way to the resting spot. She strained and could not spot anyone or anything.

She turned to survey the north side of the river, but she could not really see anything because of the cliff. She looked to the east. She was familiar with this area and knew that this river flows north after it joins the other river. She wondered how they would hide their tracks with so many horses. The men were not being careful to hide their tracks and their marks in the sand where they were making plans.

Sacred Bird surmised that they must be inviting a confrontation. She hoped they were not planning to raid another camp of her people. This thought terrified her so; she started to pray silently for her people. She did not want to witness any bloodshed. She did not want her daughter witnessing such an event. She realized then that she had completely forgotten to focus on the Creator in all the confusion.

Sacred Bird was so wrapped up in her thoughts that she did not see the leader coming toward them and gruffly motioned her to get up. She tried to get up as quickly as possible, but she was so clumsy with her wrists and ankle tied together that she fell on a rock. The pain on her right hip was so excruciating that she let out a loud cry. The man just added to her pain by kicking her thigh to get her up.

This alarmed her little daughter, and Sacred Feather Woman came running toward her, offering her mother her little hand. Sacred Bird reassured her daughter that she was all right. The man reached down and pulled Sacred Bird up to stand. but she could not stand upright, she was hunched over. She managed to hobble to where another man was waiting with a fresh horse. Her little girl was right behind her.

Sacred Feather Woman's efforts brought a lump to Sacred Bird's throat, and she could not utter a word. Sacred Feather Woman was being so grown-up in spite of all that was happening.

Sacred Bird realized she was getting emotional, and every little event touched some raw nerve, which in turn seemed to bring on the tears. She turned and quickly kissed and hugged Sacred Feather Woman before the tears came, but Sacred Feather Woman saw them and whispered, "Na'aa, it's ok."

With those words, Sacred Bird could not stop the tears. They flowed freely and she felt good to release them. She managed a smile before the man got her on the horse and the other man took Sacred Feather Woman. Sacred Bird waved to her daughter. Sacred Feather Woman gave her mother a big smile.

They headed north until they came to a place where the river changed direction to the east. The sun had set, but there was still light enough to see. Going uphill was incredibly challenging. Sacred Bird tried to hold onto the horse's mane but it was so difficult to hang on, she fell off the horse three times. Each time her body shifted, her hands would cramp up. The cramps made it more difficult to hold on.

The times she fell, she would just lie on the ground. She could not move any part of her body. The man had to practically throw her back on the horse. Hanging on was getting intolerable. Her hands and fingers would start to feel so numb from trying to hold on that it took a while before the feeling came back.

They finally reached the top of the hill. Sacred Bird was so exhausted from the falls that she almost lost consciousness. She must have because the voices she heard seemed distant and muffled. She struggled to stay conscious and stay on the horse. She could not remember, but she must have slipped into unconsciousness for a time. Sacred Feather Woman's calls brought her back to consciousness and just in time, she was about to fall again. Sacred Bird sat up and looked around, then she remembered where they were.

This part of the land was different. There were no trees to hide the group. They were out on the prairie. There were hills and small valleys with short shrubs. They could see the horizon. The men rode in silence. Sacred Feather Woman was the only one talking to her mother, but Sacred Bird could not make out what her daughter was saying. Sacred Bird tried to talk to Sacred Feather Woman, but she could not talk. Her mouth was dry and her throat was parched. Sacred Feather Woman fell silent. Sacred Bird desperately tried to regain her ability to balance her thoughts.

After a while she looked over to Sacred Feather Woman. Her daughter had fallen asleep, her head bobbing with the movement of the horse. Sacred Bird hoped her daughter would not wake up with a sore neck. Sacred Bird was glad they were not going fast. The evening air was getting cool, and she became quite concerned about her daughter's well-being. Sacred Bird started praying in her mind and asked the Creator to give them the strength to make the journey. Her mind turned to the events of the day.

She looked back to see if the other three men would be bringing the horses. They must have stayed behind in the valley by the river. As Sacred Bird was gazing toward the river, she saw the dust before she saw them.

They were coming at a fast pace. She wondered if they were being chased . . . the leader barked some words and held the rope from the horse Sacred Bird was on out to the young man who rode with Sacred Bird's daughter. The young man came alongside Sacred Bird and took the reins and the rope.

It was obvious something was happening, and Sacred Bird could not figure it out. The young man led the horse Sacred Bird was on straight ahead, while the leader and the others stayed behind. Sacred Bird's heart skipped a beat. For a moment she imagined her rescuers were just behind them, and then feared for them, supposing these men spotted them and stayed behind to ambush them.

She turned around, straining to see but it was getting too dark. The horse's pace picked up a bit and Sacred Bird crouched a little to hold onto the horse's mane better. Sacred Bird had so many questions that needed answers. She became very frustrated that she could not communicate with these men. Why would they wait back there with all those horses? She wished she could understand their language.

They rode in silence for a while. Not wanting to break that silence, Sacred Bird listened to the thudding sounds of the horses' hooves on the dry ground. The horses' heavy breathing seemed to fill the air as they made their way in the evening.

Sacred Bird could not stand the silence and called out to Sacred Feather Woman, "Sacred Feather Woman, can you hear me?"

Right away Sacred Feather Woman replied, "Yes, Na'aa."

At the same time, the young man moved the horses closer together so Sacred Bird would not have to speak in a loud voice.

"Are you tired yet? Do you have aches in your body?" Sacred bird questioned her. She was not too sure Sacred Feather Woman would understand, but it was worth a try.

Sacred Feather Woman answered. "Yes Na'aa, this hurts . . ." she said, pointing to her backside and neck.

Sacred Bird told her to have patience, "I think we should be having a rest very soon . . . then I can rub your back and you can sleep a little, ok?"

Sacred Feather Woman answered, "Ok, but then can we go home?"

Sacred Bird fell silent then, not knowing what to say or how to answer, finally she told her daughter. "We cannot go home, yet . . ."

Sacred Feather Woman interrupted and asked, "Why can't we go home?"

Sacred Bird replied confidently, "We cannot right now, not until we get to the camp of these men, then we can start back."

Even though Sacred Bird was saying more than her little Sacred Feather Woman, it felt good to hear their words. Sacred Bird thought to herself, 'we will not lose our language, no matter how long we are away, and I will make sure that little Sacred Feather Woman learns as much as I know. I will talk to her later after we have rested.'

Sacred Bird told her daughter, "We will talk some more after we stop, ok?" Sacred Feather Woman reached out to touch her mother's arm before the two horses walked apart for a few paces.

The young man suddenly motioned them to be quiet and looked back as if he could recognize what he heard. He stopped the horses and listened. It was getting dark now, but persons and other objects could still be seen up close.

Sacred Bird heard the horses approaching fast and was fearful. When she turned toward the approaching horses, she saw the dark figures. The men were softly talking, too calmly, and this puzzled her. She could not help being curious. She may never know what was going on and she felt it was important to have an idea of what was happening by knowing what or who was present.

The group caught up with them. After a while they reached a small Coulee where they stopped to rest for the night. The young man reached up and held her arm as if to tell her 'it is time to get off.' Sacred Bird let him help her off. She did not want to fall as before. She hobbled along behind him as he led Sacred Feather Woman and Sacred Bird away from the rest of the group. He directed Sacred Bird to a spot far away from the group and motioned her to sit down on the ground, indicating with his arms that this was where they would bed down for the night. Sacred Bird sat with Sacred Feather Woman on her lap.

Sacred Feather Woman started whispering questions. "Who are these people? Do you know them? Why are we stopping here? Can we go home? How long do we have to stay here?"

Sacred Bird answered as best she could, being careful not to alarm her daughter and have her cry out loud. Sacred Bird told her daughter she had to eat and then have a good rest.

Sacred Feather Woman sat and ate the meat that the young man had given them. After a while, the same young man came over and handed them a small water container and left them. The water refreshed their parched and dry throats. Sacred Bird was glad she and Sacred Feather Woman had some privacy, even for a short time.

That first night seemed like an exceptionally long night. Sacred Bird thought it would never end. Throughout the night, Sacred Bird was cold and uncomfortable. The hide that the man gave them was adequate and kept Sacred Feather Woman warm all night. Sacred Bird was not so lucky. The hide was a bit small and one side of her was warm all night, while the other side was cold. Sacred Bird did not mind, what mattered most was Sacred Feather Woman's comfort.

Sacred Bird had been lucky. She did not break any bones from the trip or from her captors. She prayed to the Creator that the men would not make any sexual advances for the remainder of the trip. She knew then she had to be incredibly careful to shield her baby from witnessing an unpleasant event and not let her guard down. That night the men did not make any fires, they sat quietly having a discussion.

The horses were snorting and moving about, perhaps it was the coyotes' howling, or perhaps it was the foxes' sharp yipping that made them restless, or maybe they sensed a long journey. There were so many sounds that night, Sacred Bird had a hard time falling asleep. Her muscles were sore from the ride, and she wanted to moan to ease the pain. As she tried to sleep, the night noises became louder and more defined, even the grass rustled loudly as it waved in the slight breeze.

Her thoughts turned to her family at the home camp. 'Are they missing us? Are my young sons going to be able to function in my absence?' She wondered when she would be able to see them again. 'Will they miss me and Sacred Feather Woman as much as we will miss them? Or are they going to go about life as if we never existed?' Sacred Bird knew this last question was not true, of course. They were going to miss them and come after them, she just did not know when.

CHAPTER 3

THE STRANGE CAMP

They had been travelling for many days; in fact the new moon had just come up. Just when Sacred Bird would sink into oblivion, her body would somehow find the strength to continue this nightmare. Her daughter was not in any better shape than her . . . Sacred Feather Woman had been unable to keep her food down. Sacred Bird worried that her daughter might not survive the journey. Not knowing where they were headed was another obstacle they had to contend with. Sacred Bird hoped they could survive the ordeal and ultimately return to their people.

Others had joined them about five days before. The number of men had increased from four to about twenty, including countless horses. It was difficult to count the number of men because some would ride away from the group while others would come. It was also difficult for Sacred Bird to know which was which. Her captors kept her and Sacred Feather Woman away from the rest of the men, who all seem uninterested in them.

Sacred Bird noticed that they must be nearing the desti-nation, as the men seemed to relax more and the rope tying her wrists to her ankle had been removed. Her captor must have been confident that she would not try to escape. He must have thought that Sacred Bird would lose her way if she tried to return on her own. He must have thought that Sacred Bird had not been paying attention and would not remember the way they came.

The terrain made Sacred Bird sick. She felt like she was being squeezed mentally, and sometimes she almost panicked. They had reached the land with more trees and uneven ground. This part of the land was rough and hilly. There were streams and ponds. There was so much water and so many insects that she feared she may become sick with the poison these insects were putting into her body.

It took all her energy to concentrate on staying on the horse. Her body could not withstand any more falls. She could not remember the number of times she had fallen off the horse since they entered the woods. She remembered the first time. She had fallen asleep as they neared the trees . . . the next instant, she found herself in a mud hole. Her captor had said some harsh-sounding words as he assisted her back on the horse while the others laughed at her. One reward from being covered in mud was that the flying insects did not bother her until the mud came off.

Sacred Bird was not too concerned about her appear-ance; in fact, the less attractive she was, the better. Her main concern was that Sacred Feather Woman stay safe through-out this journey. She made a point of knowing where her little Sacred Feather Woman was since they entered the forest. Sometimes she would lose sight of her daughter, but when she did catch a glimpse of her, Sacred Feather Woman seemed to be sleeping.

Sacred Bird prayed that was the Creator's way of allowing Sacred Feather Woman's frail body to heal despite the gruelling test the journey seemed to put on the body. She, on the other hand, was in poor shape. Although her wounds had partially healed, there were big brown scabs over most of her body, and her knees felt like they were going to buckle under her frail body. Her arms were weak; sometimes she was unable to hold Sacred Feather Woman.

The horses seemed to labour as they travelled between the trees and over marshy wet ground. One day it seemed that they went through water and did not touch dry ground until it was almost night. The men made camp, and they had a big bonfire for the first time. They were happy, talking and laughing as they ate their meal, while Sacred Bird and Sacred Feather Woman sat quietly in a makeshift shelter made of branches away from the group. Sacred Bird could not see the horses and some of the other men. She counted the men. There were only twelve men. She guessed that the other men must be tending other horses or well on their way to their home camp.

Sacred Bird tried to make sense of the trip. It seemed that thinking was all she could do. She wondered and asked the same questions. 'Why would they want a woman from our tribe? What purpose would I serve? How long have they watched the home camp? What fate awaits me at their camp? I have heard of tribes taking women from other tribes to use their skills in making the necessities of life, and others were taken to be wives of the prominent men of the tribe.'

She shuddered at the thought of being a wife to someone so different in culture and traditional ways, and someone whose language she would not understand. How would she communicate? Sign language is not enough.

That night, as in the previous nights, had sounds that were different from the night sounds of the prairies. Sacred Bird laid there holding on to Sacred Feather Woman, who had fallen asleep after a small meal. Sacred Feather Woman seemed to be better this evening. Sacred Bird hoped that whatever her daughter had before was out of her system and now she was well on the way to recovery.

Sacred Bird gazed at the sky. The stars filled the night sky. There were so many of them. She swore that if there had been more, they would knock each other out of the sky. The moon was not quite full and yet it gave out enough light for them to see quite clearly. Sacred Bird laid awake listening to the sounds of the night and looking at the stars.

Somewhere in the woods to her right, she heard the deep-throated hooting of an owl, which was answered by another off to her left. The one on the left sounded farther away than the one on the right. They hooted to each other for a while until a wolf howled, followed by others. The wolves sounded as if they were near enough that Sacred Bird could just reach out and touch them. The wolf's howls sounded fiercer than the coyote's howls. The wolf's howls were much more frightening. Sacred Bird felt uneasy. She thought she would not be able to sleep with them so close by.

Sacred Bird listened for a while. There were so many noises in the night, insects buzzing around her head, insects making rubbing sounds, frogs gurgling in the water, and the rustling of the leaves as the breeze moved through the trees. She could also hear twigs breaking in the distance and she knew it must be an animal hunting for its survival. Off in the distance she could hear the muffled music of what sounded like rushing water or maybe a waterfall.

The men hardly made any sounds except for some. Sacred Bird learned to recognize one who coughed a lot; he had a distinctive sound, it was as if his whole being was going to come out of his body. The others just moved noisily and they munched as if they were having a feast.

Sacred Bird looked up at the clear sky and studied the stars. She found the seven stars. She had found them before, but this time they seemed so close . . . suddenly she realized that they had travelled north. She had not kept track of the number of days they had travelled. She scolded herself for not keeping track of the days, but if she thought about it, she might be able to count the days. Knowing the number of days would tell her how many days it would take her and Sacred Feather Woman to get home. Her heart skipped a beat just thinking about her loved ones.

The next day the sky filled with clouds; Sacred Bird knew it was going to rain. The rain came and drenched the group and the horses. The lightning scared the horses. The men had difficulty keeping the horses calmed. Sacred Bird and Sacred Feather Woman were terrified. Sacred Bird was afraid the lightning would hit them because of the many trees, but the men brought them away from the trees. The robe they used kept her dry, but it did not keep part of her body dry. Sacred Bird's back got wet, and the cold kept her awake all night.

Fortunately, the next day was a hot day and the sun's rays quickly dried her clothing. Sacred Bird felt ill that day and she knew the illness was brought on by being cold all night. She longed to be back at the home camp. If she were, the old people would certainly not let her feel this way. They would get the medicine to prevent this illness from progressing further. She tried to remember what the medicine looked like and wondered if it grew around this area. She decided to look for a plant that looks like it and try it.

During the journey, she looked but could not find a plant that even resembled the plant that the old people used. She felt disappointed. She knew she had to do something, but what? She looked at Sacred Feather Woman and asked her how she felt. Sacred Feather Woman said that she was fine.

The next morning, Sacred Bird was awakened with the usual kick in the back. It was always the same man, he had an unusually ugly laugh. It must amuse him to kick Sacred Bird, he seemed to enjoy his cruel way of waking her each morning. The leader usually barked a few words as if to scold him and then the man would walk away as if complaining.

Sacred Bird was not sure, but she wondered why the leader was unusually protective of Sacred Bird and Sacred Feather Woman. This puzzled Sacred Bird. She wondered why she had not been abused more lately and why she had been left alone at night.

Sacred Bird and her daughter got up. She brushed the leaf and grass debris off her daughter and herself. They splashed cold water on their faces to refresh themselves and wash the sleep from their eyes. Sacred Bird dreaded this day, she knew it would be filled with the usual . . . trees, bugs, wet land, and more riding. She wanted to walk but knew she could not because of the wet land, high grass, and insects.

She had no choice but to ride the horse and hold on. This part of the country was not only filled with trees, but also hills, rivers, and lakes, which made it difficult for Sacred Bird to ride. It was a struggle to stay on. Holding on made her arms and hands numb, and that made it difficult to open her hands after being closed for so long.

She felt weak as she stood up holding onto a nearby tree, and then she felt as if the trees were being whirled around her. She closed her eyes, but she still felt as if she was being hurled into the air, so she opened her eyes. She stood for a while holding on to the tree; finally the feeling of being unsteady slowly went away. She could not understand what was happening to her, but she managed to have a clear head the rest of the day. She was sure the Creator was with her, keeping her and her daughter safe and guiding her. She was convinced that if she did not talk to the Creator, she would not survive. She must pray for the Creator's guidance and hope to survive.

The day dragged on and on, and just when she thought it would never end, they reached a big lake where she hoped they would rest. However, they were able to walk on the sandy shore. They stopped and watered the horses, but the horses seemed very uneasy as they drank the water. The men seemed concerned, and they tried their best to settle the horses. Sacred Bird tried to figure out what it was the horses were sensing . . . then suddenly the odour hit her. She looked at the men but they seemed not to notice the smell, which puzzled her.

The next part of the journey was uneventful. Sacred Bird stayed close to Sacred Feather Woman and the young man who kept her daughter safe on the long journey. He seemed to be a gentle and considerate young man, taking his duty of guarding Sacred Bird's daughter very seriously and with the leader's approval. His duty of making sure Sacred Feather Woman was safe was very much appreciated. Sacred Bird had not been able to let him know how thankful she was, so with gratitude she would present a smile towards the young man.

The men talked more and seemed more happy than usual. Sacred Bird guessed their camp must be near. One of the men rushed off ahead of them to join, as Sacred Bird guessed, the rest of the men and horses who had gone on before them. Sacred Bird again could smell the odour she had noticed at the edge of the lake. It was a bit faint, but it seemed so evil. She could not figure out what it was, but it had a rotting smell, like an old carcass of an animal.

They continued the journey through the trees, water, and gullies. Every part of Sacred Bird's body was sore, and her mind was busy with thoughts. Sometimes she tried to imagine the land she left behind, but it was difficult to imagine because of the terrain they travelled. She once tried to sing some of the happy songs from the home camp, but she could not; it seemed so out of place. At other times, she talked to the Creator out loud. No one told her to keep quiet.

At one stop, she could not control the tears. Sacred Feather Woman made a gallant effort to console her. Sacred Bird cried a long time and when she stopped, she tried to explain how she felt to Sacred Feather Woman. She felt sadness, hopelessness, helplessness, and loneliness. She had never felt these feelings all at once before and now she was being overwhelmed by them. There was no way out of this situation. After the explanation, Sacred Feather Woman held her hand and asked if they should pray.

They sat and held hands and prayed. The prayer helped Sacred Bird. She felt relieved that she had someone to console and help her pull herself together. She hugged her daughter and thanked her. She was glad to have such a caring daughter. Sacred Bird was also glad her daughter was wise for her years. Sacred Bird was able to regain her composure. They sat and talked for a while. Sacred Feather Woman said she knew they would be safe.

They sat in silence for a while before the man came with the horses and they went on their way. They rode in silence. Sacred Bird thought of the little incident and wondered how she had lost control of herself. She had always been strong, just like the women back at home camp, but their strengths had never been tested. How much can a person endure before such feelings take over and overpower with such devastating results?

They rode single file for a while through rocky terrain and trees. Sacred Bird hung on until her knuckles were white; she felt numb from her fingers down to her toes. Sometimes she would slip to the side and back of the horse when they went up and down hills, and sometimes she would crouch down to avoid getting her face scratched from the trees. She looked over at the men and wondered how they were able to ride perfectly while she was having trouble staying on the horse.

Still deep in her thoughts, they reached the top of a hill. When she looked, she saw the camps below. Looking down, she saw the people eagerly waiting for the men. They all seemed so pleased to see the men, waving and shouting as if to welcome their heroes.

Sacred Bird was not sure how to react. Reaching this camp stirred mixed emotions within her, she was not sure whether to be thankful or not. Reaching their destination may have its drawbacks but at least the journey was over, but what awaited Sacred Bird and Sacred Feather Woman?

Sacred Bird prayed silently and asked the Creator to make this place bearable until they could return home. She decided she would make plans and prepare to leave as soon as possible.

They walked the horses slowly down the hill. The others shouted and hurried down to meet the smiling faces of their loved ones. The loved ones seemed overjoyed at the return of the men, who must have been away for quite a long time. Sacred Bird was tired and sore, and she knew the horse she was on was quite tired too, so she let the horse walk. She followed at a much slower pace.

The young man who rode with her daughter steered his horse to Sacred Bird's and handed Sacred Feather Woman to her. He was eager to join the others. For a short time Sacred Bird was completely ignored, and it would have been a perfect time for her to get away, but she was so exhausted, she did not care. She had no energy to move. She held onto Sacred Feather Woman and was content to walk the horse slowly. She felt as if every part of her body was going to fall apart with each step the horse took. She stared at the others and wondered what they were going to do to her.

CHAPTER 4

NORTHERN CAMP

The camp was situated in a clearing not far from a stream or river. It was late in the day when they arrived. The sun had been beating down on them for most of the day and the flying insects had been unruly. They had no respect for anyone. The insects seemed to exist because the people were there to provide whatever nourishment they needed.

The camp had all types of tepees and shelters. They were not set in any order, they were more haphazard but in the centre was an old tepee, larger than all the others. Four men sat in front of this tepee. These men appeared to be important leaders; they waited patiently for the crowd to quiet down before one of them rose and began to speak to the leader who had captured Sacred Bird.

The journey now completed, Sacred Bird felt sick to her stomach, brought on by a combination of all the fears, both emotional and physical. She felt weak and could not make herself let go of the horse. She dreaded what was in the immediate future and did not want to deal with this strange place. It took all her strength just to get off the horse.

She took the rope that had been used to lead the horse and started to walk with her daughter still riding the horse. Sacred Bird was ready to face whatever this place would bring. Her mind told her to keep moving, but not sure where, she stopped and stood for a long time, completely ignored by everyone, until some women surrounded her, talking in their language while examining her as though she was not aware of them.

Sacred Bird had difficulty adjusting to this 'new' camp. She and Sacred Feather Woman had to struggle through more hardships of survival. This time she had to protect herself and Sacred Feather Woman emotionally. She had to preserve her dignity, such as it was. Sacred Bird struggled physically and emotionally just to hang on to her dignity. She also had to protect her daughter from any unpleasant events that were inflicted on her by the children of the camp. She had to show them that she will protect her daughter.

Life began in the strange camp, and it was quite different and difficult at times. Sacred Bird was told to follow one woman. She was one of the wives of "Man with Many Medicines". Man with Many Medicines was one of the important men in the camp, a medicine man of sorts.

Sacred Bird could not figure out who he was until an old woman attempted to tell her. Sacred Bird had great difficulty understanding the sign language. She guessed the old woman to be a relative of Man With Many Medicines. The Old Woman seemed to have a high regard for him, just as the other members of the community did.

Sacred Bird later learned that Man with Many Medicines had four wives, all different ages. The youngest must be younger than Sacred Bird. All were extremely hard workers and went out of their way to please the man. They kept Sacred Bird in line by ordering her to work just as hard as they did, although Sacred Bird seemed to do the more strenuous chores. She did not mind the hard physical labour, it took her mind off her predicament and helped to pass the time more quickly.

The most difficult change in her life was the food, which was entirely different than the food back home. Sacred Bird was not used to the food and most of the time she usually became sick; she lost a lot of weight.

A typical day started before sunrise. Sacred Bird learned to do her chores before she was told to do them. Her chores were gathering firewood and fetching the water for the morning, midday, and evening meals and sometimes in the night. In between the meals, she cleaned the tepees; there were three tepees that needed cleaning.

The other wives, as she understood, told her that there will be a fourth tepee. The three tepees were getting a bit crowded. Other chores included helping with the skinning, tanning, and making of clothing and footwear out of the small animal hides. There were also larger animal hides that needed to be prepared for suitable items such as shelter, clothing, and footwear.

Gathering firewood and fetching the water were simple tasks; however, cleaning the tepees involved a lot more physical labour, like lifting and carrying the heavy bedding and animal rugs and beating them until they were clean enough. Sometimes the other wives, especially the older wives, would not be satisfied with Sacred Bird's work, and they let her know in no uncertain terms. Sometimes Sacred Bird was slapped and beaten with long twigs. There was hardly a day that went by when she wouldn't get a beating for something she did or did not do.

It was while Sacred Bird was gathering the wood or fetching the water that she would pray. She would go as often as she could just to be alone with nature and the Creator. The other women must have noticed, because one day she received a severe beating. She was beaten with sticks, which left huge welts on her legs and arms. She was at a point where she did not care; she was able to shut out the pain by concentrating on the Creator. She did not dare fight back for fear of retaliation against her daughter.

That first year with the people at the camp was exceedingly difficult in all aspects of her life. Sacred Bird not only could not understand their language, she had a difficult time with their sign language, but the women did not have patience with her.

The only one who had the time and patience was the old woman, whom everyone called "Ko'kom". Ko'kom took the time to teach Sacred Bird a few of the words using objects and repeating the words until Sacred Bird could say them. She was a kind and gentle person and she loved to laugh. Sacred Bird looked forward to the times she could spend with Ko'kom, because those were the times Sacred Bird spent with Sacred Feather Woman also.

Ko'kom had a gentle but persuasive way with the other women, and they did not dare go against her wishes.

Ko'kom would wave them away and spoke very rapidly when they came to talk with her. Later Sacred Bird found out they had come to tell her that Sacred Bird was needed for a certain chore. Sacred Bird did not mind the workload that awaited her after the sessions with Ko'kom. Working a little longer gave her a chance to repeat the words so she could remember them and associate them with words in her language. She also used the time to communicate with the Creator and to give thanks for the good health she and Sacred Feather Woman had been enjoying.

Sacred Feather Woman had an easier time with the people. She had learned the language and had started to communicate with the other children. She had also got along with them. Children are so innocent, and they do not seem to know the difference in people or tribes. They accept each other as they are and even learn to communicate in their own way.

Sacred Feather Woman spent a lot of time with the Elders and the other children. Once, Sacred Bird observed the Elders and children. They were gathered in a circle, and they were laughing and talking and playing a game. Sacred Bird wished she knew what they were laughing about, she wished she could understand the language and was a bit envious.

There were times Sacred Bird felt so alone, and she would think about the loved ones back at her home camp. It was during these times she felt as though the only one who understood her feelings was the Creator. She cried a river of tears; each time she cried, she felt her strength renewed. She tried not dwell on these thoughts and instead communicated with the Creator.

She would ask the Creator to help her find a way to return home. It was during the times she was in the woods and by the water that she felt the Creator was listening. She felt so close to the Creator, as though she could reach out and touch Him. Also, at these times she noticed that she had a follower. She never saw the person or thing that followed her everywhere she went. She assumed it was one of the women spying on her.

She guessed she had been followed for a long time, even a few moons, maybe two or three moons. It was during that time that the man came to her in the night. That night resulted in her being a complete outcast from the rest of the wives. They must have known about that night because they treated her worse than ever before. They beat her more often with sticks and demanded more work from her.

Sacred Bird did not dare slow down with her chores; she toiled from the time she got up until the time she went to sleep. She still had her times with the old woman. The old woman's attitude toward Sacred Bird did not change; Ko'kom was still gentle and kind towards her.

Sacred Bird went about her chores and still communicated with the Creator even after she became with child. The work she did was not altered in any way and she managed to do them. The only difference was the beatings stopped and she was thankful, but no one told her to slow down with the chores; she was expected to do a full day's work.

Sacred Feather Woman noticed her mother's body was different. She asked questions, and although Sacred

Bird tried to answer, the old woman answered her. Sacred Feather Woman was not four winters old when she was given a lesson on life. Sacred Bird listened with interest as the old woman told her stories about life and nature and the purpose of new life. Sacred Bird understood little of what she said, but Sacred Feather Woman understood. She in turn recounted what was said so that Sacred Bird could also hear the stories. Sacred Bird was amazed at the old woman's wisdom. Sacred Feather Woman was fortunate to have such a good teacher.

That winter was very cold, with more snow than Sacred Bird had ever seen. The cold north wind blew, and it was very hard to see, even during the day. During the days, no one ventured outside except for a few. She heard what sounded like praying and singing in the other tepees, but she could not understand. The ceremonies would go on and on throughout most of the day. She was beginning to see strange things and hear strange noises. Sacred Bird thought she was being haunted by her own thoughts and resolved not to lose her sanity. She would silently pray in her mind not to be overcome by these strange events.

After the winter had passed and spring was about to bring new life, Sacred Bird gave birth to a baby boy. She had mixed emotions about this baby, but in time she learned to accept this baby boy and not see him as a hindrance to her escape from the camp. Before she gave birth, there was a form of celebration that Man with Many Medicines had with some of the other men in the camp. They held their celebration in another man's tepee. Sacred Bird heard their singing, prayers, and chants while she was about to give birth. Four old women, including Ko'kom, tended to her.

She felt this birth was easier than her first three. She was in the usual pain and instead of screaming, she prayed out loud asking for mercy and a quick birth. She did not want the women to have the satisfaction of seeing her in great pain. She ignored them when they urged her to bite on a rawhide, as if it would ease the pain.

The birth of her son came after a long time. Sacred Bird was exhausted and felt like she was drifting away into a deep and peaceful sleep. She would have if the women had not kept her from drifting off with gentle slaps and calls. They stayed with her throughout the night.

That next evening, there was a great celebration. It seemed as if the whole camp was there. There was a bonfire, singing, and dancing. The men of importance all sat together. The people celebrated long into the night. Sacred Bird did not stay long; she was still exhausted and was thankful to drift off into a much-needed sleep.

The next day she felt strong enough to venture into a new day with her new child. She did not have a name yet and was sure a name would be given in the very near future by some Elder. The older wives took her new child; she could see her child only long enough to feed him and then they took him. She knew then that she would not be raising her son.

Giving birth did not excuse her from the strenuous chores that needed to be done. She was expected to do most of them. She noticed that the youngest wife was given some of the chores she had been doing and hoped that the young woman had the stamina to do them. The young woman had given birth the previous summer and had a hard time with childbirth. She was the only one, besides the old woman, who seemed happy for Sacred Bird. The young woman kept talking and laughing. Sacred Bird laughed with her, even though she did not understand what the young woman was laughing about. Sacred Bird just wanted to laugh because it felt good to laugh.

One day, while Sacred Bird was in the woods picking berries with the other women, she saw a man who seemed vaguely familiar. He was with some other women and children. Sacred Bird must have been staring at him for some time before he noticed and stared back at her. Sacred Bird was a little embarrassed. Without thinking, she spoke in her language to him. To Sacred Bird's surprise, he understood her and told her his name was Eagle Crier. Sacred Bird had never heard of him, but she was thankful for someone who spoke her language.

Eagle Crier told her that he could not spend too much time talking with her because he was afraid of Man with Many Medicines. He turned and walked away before Sacred Bird could ask him how he came to be at this camp. There were so many questions she wanted to ask him but could not. She stood there watching him walk away toward a pretty girl with a small baby. Sacred Bird assumed the pretty girl must be his wife.

It was many days later that Sacred Bird saw Eagle Crier again. This time he asked who her people were. Sacred Bird told him, Akainaiwa. He told her that he and his family planned to return to his people before the leaves fall and wanted to know if she wanted to send any messages. Sacred Bird told him she was not going to send messages; that she was going home on her own or with him. He looked alarmed and told Sacred Bird that Man with Many Medicines had many powerful medicines. Eagle Crier was afraid to help Sacred Bird leave the camp.

Eagle Crier told her he would not let her come along with him and his family and would not discuss it any further. Sacred Bird assured him that she was not afraid, and this was her chance to return. Sacred Bird vowed that no one was going to prevent her from going home. She was determined to go.

Deep inside, Sacred Bird was overjoyed but she could not show it. She had to keep her feelings hidden. She tried not to show it, but the feeling of gladness made her feel like jumping and shouting. Instead she bit her lip and pinched herself. She had to keep the feeling of joy inside and must not show it in any way.

Sacred Bird felt such joy, as if an invisible robe had been lifted from her shoulders. She could finally breathe and relax knowing that she would soon be able to walk with pride. She did not fully understand this invisible robe that surrounded her, but it was stifling her. She longed to find the dignity she had lost and find the true happiness of being herself. She longed to find the beauty in her surroundings again. She must have stood there for a very long time when she realized that she was being called. The calling brought her back to the camp and reality.

Sacred Bird did not know how she would prepare for the escape. She prayed and waited for a sign from the Creator.

Within the next few days, she was shown her way of escape in a dream. In the dream, she was running in the forest. She did not know what she was running from, but she knew she had to avoid certain obstacles that were in her path. She knew that if these obstacles touched her, she would not be able to escape. Her dream was in total darkness except for the immediate few steps ahead of her. The escape was made more difficult with the load she was carrying. She saw a light in the distance, which she gathered to be her destination; that was what she was aiming for.

When she awoke the next morning, she could still see the light. She did not know what her dream meant, and she could not go to anyone to find out its meaning. In the next few days, her thoughts always turned to that dream when she thought about the journey home. She wondered if the dream meant that the journey home would be impossible. Sacred Bird struggled with her thoughts and finally turned to the Creator. She could not begin to hope without trusting in the Creator. Sacred Bird made a point to go into the woods every chance she could to pray and ask for guidance.

CHAPTER 5

PREPARING FOR THE JOURNEY SOUTH

*S*acred Bird went about the preparation blindly not knowing how she was going to go. All she knew was that she was determined to go. The obstacles did not matter, as long as she could take her daughter with her.

During the meals she took more food and dried meat than she could eat, half of which she would hide in a pouch. Then, whenever she had the chance, she would hide the pouch in a tree in the forest, well above the reach of small animals and wolves. She was not too sure of the birds; if they got to the food and ate some, she would share with them. She repaired and hid a pair of old moccasins and spare clothing.

She also hid some spare moccasins and clothing for her daughter. After a few days, she had managed to hide four pouches, each in a different place. She had also managed to tie each in such a way that would be easy to take down without too much trouble and in less time. Each day she was in the woods she would look up at the hiding places but did not dare take the items down for fear that someone might be watching and discover her secret hiding places. The next few days she did not know what condition the food was in. She would not know until she took the pouches down for the journey.

The days were getting shorter, and the leaves were changing their colours. She knew the time for the journey was nearing. At times, she could not contain her excitement. She felt like running through the woods and shouting to let all the animals know that her freedom was at hand, but of course she did not. She could not even utter a word out loud or let her excitement show lest the people guess. Sometimes keeping the secret made her feel like others could see that she was hiding something. That feeling of being transparent made her feel weak and would almost make her lose her balance. The secret also made her heart race and feel like it would emerge out of her chest. Other times she felt like her heart was beating next to her throat and everyone could see it thumping against her throat. It took her a long time to calm down and go about her daily chores.

One evening at a successful hunt celebration, she saw Eagle Crier and his wife, but she did not speak to him. She thought it would be best not to tell him of her plans until the very day they leave. She knew he was afraid of Man with Many Medicines and did not dare jeopardize her only way out. She planned to follow him and his family until a great distance was travelled from this camp before she made her presence known and they could not chase her back.

Sacred Bird contemplated that day and hoped it would be easier if Man with Many Medicines was conveniently away from the camp for a few days. She did not know how she could find out until she thought of Ko'kom. Ko'kom would know when Man with Many Medicines would be away. She also thought of the many ways of asking Ko'kom but could not come up with a way to ask, not having a full knowledge of the language and without raising suspicion.

Sacred Bird decided she would tell Sacred Feather Woman to ask Ko'kom how long Man with Many Medicines would be away when he leaves. There was no easy way to get Sacred Feather Woman to ask Ko'kom what she wanted to know. In a roundabout way, Sacred Bird talked with Sacred Feather Woman in private before Ko'kom came. But she did not tell her why. She instructed Sacred Feather Woman to tell Ko'kom that she was curious as to why the men leave. Sacred Bird hoped Ko'kom would dismiss this as a question that children ask and was not something important.

The prospect of leaving this place made her sad because of her son. She did not want to leave him, but she was not given a choice. Her son was taken from her since the day he was born. She often looked at him with an ache in her heart. She was not given a chance to get close to him. Even though he was only a few moons old, he did not look at Sacred Bird the way his eyes remained fixed on the older wife of Man with Many Medicines. Sacred Bird prayed to the Creator and hoped that someday her son would somehow know the truth.

The morning dew was still on the ground when Sacred Bird went outside to begin her chores. She heard a commotion next to the tepee in the centre of the camp. She looked and saw the men gathering and preparing their horses as if they were leaving on a long trip. The voices of the women and children suggested that they were saying farewell. She knew then that this must be the day she anticipated. She looked towards Eagle Crier's tepee and saw that it was gone. She was astonished at herself; how could she have missed seeing him leave?

She walked over to Ko'Kom's tepee. As she neared, she heard voices inside and waited for a short while before she made her presence known. Sacred Bird tapped on the flap. Ko'kom answered the tapping in a loud voice and in her language, which Sacred Bird perceived to be an invitation to enter. She entered the tepee.

Man with Many Medicines was seated a few feet away from Ko'kom, who was seated on the right side of the tepee. Sacred Bird was at a loss for words. Ko'kom smiled, and with her hands she told Sacred Bird to sit next to her. Sacred Bird managed a smile and sat down beside Ko'kom close to the entrance.

She sat there almost frozen with embarrassment and uneasiness. Ko'kom just sat there conversing with Man with Many Medicines and handing out little bundles to him, which he carefully packed in a larger pouch.

After a while, Ko'kom and Man with Many Medicines said their prayers. Sacred Bird sat there with her eyes closed as she said her own prayers in her mind. She did not dare look at them, waiting until she thought they were finished before she opened her eyes.

When Sacred Bird opened her eyes, she saw Man with Many Medicines had already gotten up. Sacred Bird thought she had to stand up, so she quickly got up. Sacred Bird had never been allowed to be present at one of these meetings and she did not know the proper etiquette. She stood there for a while. Man with Many Medicines had noticed that she too was standing and gave her a glare she had never seen, so she sank back down. Sacred Bird lowered her head and did not dare look at either of them.

Sacred Bird sat there waiting for Ko'kom and Man with Many Medicines to finish their conversation and finally was able to relax after he left. Ko'kom touched her arm and with a smile made sign language. What she could understand was that she wanted to share a meal together. Sacred Bird smiled and Ko'kom gave her food.

After they ate, Ko'kom talked and Sacred Bird smiled and nodded. Sacred Bird did not have a clue what Ko'kom was talking about without the sign language. Sacred Bird had forgotten why she had come to Ko'kom's tepee. She sat there and waited for Ko'kom to tell her to get to work.

She liked Ko'kom, she was such a gentle and caring woman. Ko'kom smiled and, in sign language, told her to go to work. Sacred Bird left Ko'kom's tepee feeling very down about not being able to understand more of Ko'kom's language.

She hurried to do her chores, and in her haste she tripped over a twig and fell. Her dress was covered with dead grass; as she was brushing it off, she felt someone watching her. She looked in the direction and the older wife of Man with Many Medicines was glaring at her and shaking her head.

The other women saw her clumsiness and did not waste time in letting her know.

Sacred Bird received welts on her legs from the whippings and was thankful she did not get any on her arms and hands. That was a mild beating compared to the other times she was whipped with the long thin twigs. Sacred Bird tried to calm down and not seem too anxious to finish her chores, but to do them in her 'normal' time.

She headed to the forest to gather the firewood and take time to talk with the Creator. This time she asked Him outright to help her escape with Sacred Feather Woman without arousing too much suspicion. She also asked for time to put enough distance between them and the camp. She asked for strength to be able to carry Sacred Feather Woman if a horse could not be secured for the journey.

Planning the escape and carrying out the plans were two different things, and Sacred Bird had not thought about how difficult the escape would be. She planned, in her mind, the possible steps she might take when it was time to leave. She planned to tell Sacred Feather Woman to go with her to the woods. The plan was to ask Sacred Feather Woman to help her with the chores and maybe her daughter would enjoy the walk in the woods.

Each night, whenever Sacred Bird went outside, she would study the stars in the sky and come to know the bright and not so bright ones. In her observation, she came to realize that the bright stars seem to guard an unseen animal or object. The stars have a place in the sky that never changes except to turn a little. She prayed the stars would lead them home. She remembered which stars she had observed when they first came on this journey.

One night as she stood outside, the second wife, who was not as mean as the older, came out and spoke to her. Even though Sacred Bird could not fully understand what the second wife was saying, she knew this wife had some knowledge of the stars in the sky. The second wife pointed straight above them and motioned with her hands in a circular motion and held herself and shivered. Sacred Bird assumed the woman was telling her that winter would be coming. Sacred Bird nodded and pretended to know what the woman was saying. The second wife smiled and patted Sacred Bird's shoulder and went back inside the tepee.

Sacred Bird stood there for a while longer, just breathing the night air. For the first time in a long while, she noticed the smells and the sounds of the night air. She had not taken the time to appreciate her surroundings in a long time. She heard laughter from the tepees, the dogs settling down for the night, the owls exchanging owl words, and somewhere deep in the woods she heard a sound she had not heard before. It had a deep-throated gruff sound, like it could come from a large animal. She pondered about the strange sound but pushed it out of her mind, thinking she might be able to figure it out later. Then she noticed the smell of burning wood coming from the tepees, the smell of food, and she especially liked the smell of the pine trees.

The nights were becoming cooler and crisp. She looked up at the tall trees and noticed the dancing lights above the camp. She had seen these lights before back at the home camp, but they were so far away then. She never thought she would ever be standing underneath them. The lights were so pretty, some pretty blues with a tinge of pink. She stood there beside the tepee fascinated with the lights and did not hear the women calling her. When she did hear them, she called out to them in her language without thinking, "Ah saa," to let them know she was still just outside. Reluctantly, she decided to go back in and get ready for a good night's rest.

She awoke to the noise of the children playing outside the tepee. The morning was early yet, and she wondered why the children were out so early. She sat up and looked around, the women in the tepee were still sleeping soundly and the tepee was cold. The fire had died. She decided she would get the wood and prepare the fire and warm the tepee.

She nudged Sacred Feather Woman to wake up and whispered in her ear, "Sacred Feather Woman, wake up and come with me to the water."

Sacred Feather Woman sat up and rubbed her eyes. She was about to lay back down when Sacred Bird whispered to her, "Don't go back to sleep, wake up and come with me to the stream." Her daughter slowly got up, rubbed her eyes, yawned, and followed her mother out of the tepee.

As they stepped out into the cold morning, Sacred Bird stood for a moment looking at the sun's rays which could be seen above the trees. She suddenly knew what she had to do. She hurried and gathered a few sticks and put them by the entrance to the tepee and took the water containers to fetch the water. She did her chores and had the fire going in the tepee. She took Sacred Feather Woman's hand and told her to hurry and headed for the woods. She stood for a moment and looked back at the camp.

The air was crisp; she could very faintly see her breath. Looking around at the woods, for the first time she noticed how tall the trees were and how thick the forest was. She had walked through these trees and did not notice how tall some of them were and how close together they were. She knew the paths leading in and out of the camp clearing. She spent most of her time wandering through these woods.

She had found some hiding places and had also found a spot along the river where beautiful flowers grew in abundance. That was where she usually conversed with the Creator. 'I will miss this spot, it is a spot where I grew close to my Creator,' she thought to herself.

She thought about the people who were very nice to her, the people who made her stay here bearable and who made her believe there were good people along with people who were not so good. She knew she would miss them and wondered if they would miss her. She shook her head and told herself, 'I should prepare to go.'

She led Sacred Feather Woman down the path towards her secret hiding places. Sacred Feather Woman must have sensed urgency in her mother's walk; she did not ask any questions, she just followed.

As they neared the first hiding place, Sacred Bird whispered to Sacred Feather Woman. "Do not say anything or make any noise . . . I will explain everything later."

Sacred Feather Woman nodded and followed. Sacred Bird climbed the tree and took the first bundle down. The next hidden pouch was quite far from the first hiding place, so they walked in silence.

'The forest seems a little too quiet,' she thought to herself. Sacred Bird surveyed her surroundings and did not see anything. They reached the next two hiding places and took the bundles.

They had put some distance between them and the camp when Sacred Bird was finally able to tell Sacred Feather Woman of her plan. They reached a clearing and debated whether they should cross or go around. They decided to cross the clearing to save time. They reached the other side without incident and breathed a sigh of relief.

As they walked quickly through the woods, Sacred Feather Woman turned to her mother and said, "I'm getting tired, are we going to rest soon?"

Sacred Bird told her, "Not yet, let us go a little further, then we will have a short rest." Sacred Bird looked for a good spot to rest and could not find any. She did not know what kind of a spot she was looking for.

Sacred Bird decided to carry Sacred Feather Woman on her back for a little while. It was midday when they finally found a good spot. It was at the edge of a small clearing, and Sacred Bird had a good view of the way they came. They sat down and chewed on some dried meat to replenish their strength. Sacred Feather Woman had almost dozed off when Sacred Bird gently nudged her daughter and let her know it was time to go.

So far they had not encountered any problems. Sacred Bird took the time to thank the Creator and ask for strength and the endurance to keep going. She figured they had to make up at least three days in order to catch up with Eagle Crier and his wife. They made good progress that first day. They hardly talked or made any noise.

With each step, Sacred Bird was aware of her surroundings and the noises of her surroundings. At times she heard strange noises in the woods, and each time she heard them she would walk a little faster. They also encountered the flying insects, the ones called 'narrow nosed', the ones she dreaded. She decided to cover their heads with the twigs, hoping the leaves would 'shoo' the flying insects away.

Sacred Bird did not know how far they had travelled when they came upon a wetland. She stood there trying to figure out the best way to cross it when she noticed movement in the forest across the wetland. She thought it might be an animal and thought it would not bother them if they did not bother it. She hoped it would be a harmless animal such as a deer. She decided to go around the water. They walked a great distance before they finally reached the other side, by that time the sun had moved a little more to the west. She decided to rest a short while and let Sacred Feather Woman sleep.

Off to her left, she heard a gruff and deep-throated sound, the same sound she had heard before at the camp. Now she felt afraid. It sounded too near, so she gently shook Sacred Feather Woman's shoulders and whispered, "It is time to leave, wake up . . . don't make any noise."

Sacred Feather Woman woke up and mumbled some not-so-audible words. Sacred Bird helped her daughter up and took the pouches. She told her daughter. "If you want, I could carry you until you fully wake up."

Sacred Feather Woman replied, "I can walk; it will help me wake up more."

They headed through the forest. Sacred Bird started to pray to the Creator to walk with them. She knew then that she was afraid of the animal that made the gruff and deep-throated sound.

She prayed for a safe place to spend the night and protection from the animals of the night. As they walked, she wondered if they were ever going to catch up with Eagle Crier and his wife. It might be possible, although she did not know Eagle Crier's wife. She knew that his wife appeared to be somewhat of a delicate woman. She had given birth to their first child not one winter ago.

Still deep in her thoughts, she stumbled over a tree root which may have been uncovered by too many animals going through. She suddenly realized it was getting dark, and the trail the animals made would be dangerous, so Sacred Bird stopped and listened.

The usual sounds filled the evening air. She leaned down and almost whispered, "Sacred Feather Woman, let us look for shelter or make a shelter for the night before it gets too dark out, ok?"

Sacred Feather Woman looked up at her mother and replied. "Yes, let's. I want to help you build it."

"Ok," Sacred Bird answered, "We will go into the woods and look for a good place."

They entered the woods to the right and proceeded to look for a 'good place'. Unsure what a good place would look like, Sacred Bird searched for it anyway.

After a while they found a big rock nestled against a small hill. She knew this must be the 'good place', so she told Sacred Feather Woman to start piling some small tree branches for a bed. She took her knife and proceeded to cut a big branch from a nearby tree and pulled it down until it broke away. Preparing a safe place for the night took some time; it was dark by the time they finished.

Sacred Bird felt protected as they prepared to rest for the night. She had placed the large branches into the ground and made each branch lean against the large rock. She made the covering with different sized branches and twigs with the leaves still on them to keep out the cold night air. Both were exhausted and Sacred Bird knew this was a 'good place'.

CHAPTER 6

THE SEARCH FOR EAGLE CRIER

*S*acred Feather Woman woke her mother that first morning away from the camp. Sacred Bird had not slept very well. The night was filled with more strange noises, and she felt very uneasy and scared. The sound of footsteps, twigs and leaves crackling under someone's foot, or an animal's steps were the ones that scared her the most. She did not know if the person or animal was spying on them. Or maybe the animal was considering them for its next meal.

Sacred Feather Woman said she was very cold and asked if Sacred Bird could warm her by building a fire. Sacred Bird told her daughter that it might be too soon to build a fire; they might not be far enough from the camp.

Sacred Bird explained that they were going back to their home camp in the south, that the people in the camp they had just come from might be coming after them to bring them back. Just talking about the home camp excited her. She longed to be there with family and friends. She drew the small robe around Sacred Feather Woman and hugged her. She reassured her daughter that she would warm up in a little while.

They ate a small amount of the food from the pouches. After they ate, Sacred Bird packed the robes and the food and secured the four pouches. She tied them together as she did before and headed out. They headed straight south through the forest. They saw a fox on the way, which delighted Sacred Feather Woman. Other small animals avoided them by running in the opposite direction. Just as they got comfortable with their pace, they came upon rough terrain. They could not avoid this rough terrain so they did the best they could to get through it.

The terrain was a mixture of marsh, mud, and forest undergrowth. This area had water plants, frogs, and insects. Sacred Bird carried Sacred Feather Woman on her back, the four pouches slung across her shoulders. She walked laboriously through this marshy part of the woods for much of the day. She did not mind her feet getting wet; she figured she could dry them after they reached dry ground.

Sacred Bird could not take the load off her shoulders; she did not dare risk Sacred Feather Woman's health and getting the contents of the pouches wet. She would stop and rest, standing and shifting her weight alternately on one foot then the other. This seemed to help her legs and feet, but it did not do her back and shoulders any good.

Her shoulders were starting to ache and there was a burning ache just below the back of her neck. The only way to ease the pain was to stretch her arms and then let them hang on her side. To ease the neck pain, she held her head as far back as possible, being careful not to force Sacred Feather Woman off her back. Then she would go slowly. Once, her left foot slipped and she almost fell over but managed to keep from falling, but the slip injured the back of her leg; with each step, it hurt more.

It was past midday before they finally reached dry land. By then Sacred Bird was so exhausted, wet, and sleepy from the trek. She could not move and just laid there on the ground for a long while. Sacred Feather Woman was so exhausted and tired from hanging on that she too just laid there and did not move. They were too tired to eat, they just did not have the energy to eat or talk. They laid there in silence. Sacred Bird did not want to fall asleep, they had to keep going. The only way she could muster up enough energy was to pray for strength. So she prayed. She and Sacred Feather Woman both fell asleep.

Sacred Bird woke up when she heard someone call her; she sat up and looked around. Most of the day had gone and it would be getting dark soon. She allowed Sacred Feather Woman to sleep a little before she woke her up. Sacred Bird sat there and looked at her surroundings. She thought she must have dreamt that someone called her, so she did not dwell on it.

The place where they rested seemed so peaceful, the leaves were rustling and there was a slight breeze. The sun's rays had warmed them and the air was fresh with the smell of pine. She laid back down for a while to take in the surroundings, thinking about the journey ahead of them. She shook her head. 'I should not dwell on it; hearing someone calling is not good,' she thought to herself.

Sacred Feather Woman woke up and asked for water. Sacred Bird searched the pouch, but she could not find the small water container. It must have dropped in the marsh when she almost slipped. Sacred Bird told her daughter to get ready to go, that they would have to search for water before they stopped for the night. She knew there must be a stream or a river because they had crossed countless lakes and rivers on the way during the first journey. They got up and gathered the pouches. Sacred Feather Woman offered to carry one pouch, so Sacred Bird gave her the lightest one.

They headed south through the woods. It was almost sunset when they reached a river. They had passed a small pond, but it was not good to drink, it was too still. They came upon the river which was down a large coulee. Sacred Bird could see far from this vantage point. She saw four deer down at the river's edge, so she knew it must be safe to go down there.

Sacred Feather Woman was impatient to go down and was not careful with her first step down the steep hill. She slipped and fell and scraped her hand. The scrape was not too bad, just scratched, and she was able to keep from crying. She amazed her mother, but her pride had been wounded.

"Are you hurt?" Sacred Bird asked as she leaned down to help her daughter up.

"No, I think I scraped my hands . . . Ow! My elbow hurts, too," Sacred Feather Woman said.

"Come . . . take my hand, we will go down together. We have to step very carefully, this hill is too steep to rush down," she told her daughter as she took Sacred Feather Woman's hand and carefully stepped down the hill. "We cannot risk falling . . . it will be too painful to fall, and we will fall really far."

They took care with each step and managed to reach the river without incident. They drank their fill and sat on a big rock to rest before they looked for a place to cross the river. Sacred Bird wished they had a horse. A horse would have made a difference. She thought about how she was going to cross the river without getting the pouches wet. They walked along the river's edge before they found a place to cross. There was a shallow part, but it was very rocky. Sacred Bird needed something to help keep her balanced while crossing the river with the load. She looked and found a long branch.

She carried her daughter on her back, the four pouches slung over her shoulders. She took each step very carefully, making sure her feet would not slip on the rocks.

The crossing was difficult, and she could feel her body beginning to ache. She had strained her body from the load and felt very tired. She told Sacred Feather Woman that they had to sit and rest for a while. She sat down and examined her feet for any blisters. She was glad she did not have any. As she sat there, she looked at the food and knew that there would be enough food for the journey if they travelled at an even pace.

Sacred Feather Woman wandered off to explore the surroundings. Sacred Bird told her daughter that the journey would be tiring, so she would have to help by keeping up and not wandering off each time they stopped. She told her daughter they would have to conserve their energy for the journey.

Sacred Bird knew she was being a little hard on Sacred Feather Woman by asking her not to look around, so she explained that they had to make it to the home camp before the snow flies. Sacred Bird had a feeling that the snow might come earlier than she had anticipated. The air had more coolness than the days before, and she had seen the big birds flying south in formation earlier that day. She had also noticed that the small animals had scurried about, gathering their food for the coming of winter.

After a short rest, Sacred Bird told her daughter to take a drink of water before they started out. They had no water container. She searched the pouches for something to carry a small amount of water. She took the hide which wrapped the food they had consumed and hoped it would hold the water. The wrapping was able to hold a small amount. She secured the water by tying the top with the tie from her braid. She did not need to braid her hair anyway.

Sacred Bird surveyed their surroundings before they headed out. The only movements and noises came from the birds and small animals. She looked up at the sky. There were a few clouds, and the sun would be setting soon. They headed up the steep hill. This side had more small bushes than the other side, so they hung on each little bush to pull themselves up. Sacred Feather Woman followed behind her mother. They made good time. Using the bushes made the climb up the hill easier.

They reached the top and rested just for a short while. Sacred Bird surveyed the distant land. She could see far from this spot and saw that the land ahead of them looked tiresome. The land ahead of them consisted of trees, bushes, and rolling hills. Sacred Bird said a short prayer for strength and good weather, and most of all to find Eagle Crier and his family before going on. She took Sacred Feather Woman's hand and led her through some small bushes, being careful not to let the small branches slap her daughter's face.

The sun had gone down, but it was still light enough for them to see where they were going. They travelled over two hills before Sacred Bird decided to rest and make a shelter for the night. This part of the land had few trees, but many small bushes. She took her knife and started making the shelter with the small bushes. It was almost dark before she finished.

The nights were getting colder, and she decided to make a small fire. Without the moon's light it was hard to see. The moon would not be in the sky for a few more days. That night Sacred Bird and Sacred Feather Woman sat and talked for a while before they went to sleep. Sharing information was becoming a good habit, even the dreams each had.

Sacred Bird could not sleep. She got up to feed the fire before it went out. Her thoughts turned to her loved ones at the home camp. She wondered which place the camp was moved to. She began to recount the past moves and knew that the camp must be near the mountains by now. That would be the most logical place because of the shelter and game. The bison must also be near the hills. She hoped she would find the home camp when they got there. Then she thought of the many camps that would be scattered throughout the land. She knew she would be able to find her family.

She had just begun to fall asleep when she heard noises in the distance. She sat up and listened. The night air was cool and crisp, she could see her breath. She turned toward the noise. The noise was coming from the direction they had come from. She recognized the sounds she had heard before. She decided to add to the fire just in case the animal or animals came.

It seemed like the noises were coming closer. With the noises, she could also hear the wolves off to the west. She did not worry about the wolves; she felt she could deal with them if they came. It was the noises that were coming closer she had to worry about. The usual night noises like the owl and the fox had stopped. She listened and then she remembered. The noises were not real but were spirits. She tried to remember exactly when she had started to hear these noises.

Then she remembered. It was one night back at the camp of Man with Many Medicines that she first heard these noises. She had gone to bed and the people at the camp had settled in for the night. They were coming from Man With Many Medicines' lodge one night. He had a few of the men in his lodge when they began chanting and singing their ceremonial songs.

She had been curious about their ceremony and had slipped out into the night to listen in secret. She thought she saw the spirits. She had not seen their faces but their forms, and there were many. They had terrified her then, because she did not know what they were. When she saw them, she froze, unable to move. At the time she did not know how long she had remained in the same spot, but she had managed to get back to her bed. She could not sleep that night; the sight had made her body weak . . . the noises had been eerie.

The spirits arrived and began circling their little shelter. Sacred Bird felt some coming closer, so close that she felt a rush of air pass by her ear and almost pulled her cover off. She could hear the flames roar amid the noise and then the sound of sparks. When she heard the flames roar, she felt a searing pain shoot through her body, and she dared not cry out in pain. The pains felt like something was piercing her skin. Thinking fast, she shielded Sacred Feather Woman with her body and tried to keep her daughter's eyes covered.

Sacred Bird remained awake that night. Her only defence was prayer, so she spent most of the night praying with her eyes closed, holding Sacred Feather Woman close. She was afraid to open her eyes for fear that she would be over-powered by them. One time she thought the spirits were taunting her in her language. She did not know if she was imagining it, but she thought she heard the words so clear. She was quite sure they said that she could not escape and that her journey had already been cursed. That unless she returned, she would not be safe. At another time, she was sure she felt herself being lifted into the air and dropped.

Even though she was terrified, she kept on praying; sometimes she would pray out loud, almost shouting, to drown out the horrible noises. With her eyes closed, she would sing her prayers until she became hoarse and could not shout above a loud whisper. At times she cried and asked the Creator to rescue her from this terrible ordeal. She prayed for daylight to come. The spirits finally disappeared as daylight came. She was so thankful to the Creator for keeping her from being overpowered. She prayed that the spirits would not return the next night.

Sacred Bird was wide awake the next morning. She gently shook Sacred Feather Woman to wake her. She asked her daughter if she remembered the events of the night. Sacred Feather Woman said she did not hear anything. Sacred Bird was puzzled by this. She remembered hearing her daughter cry out after each hard landing from being lifted up. Sacred Bird wanted to be sure her daughter really did not hear the events and noises of the night before.

Sacred Feather Woman reassured her mother, saying, "I did not hear any noise. I was sleeping."

Sacred Bird decided not to dwell on the matter, even though she could not erase the event from her mind. She got up to feed the fire and warm up. She took the food from the pouches, and they ate and drank the water. She told Sacred Feather Woman to get up and put her moccasins on for the journey. Sacred Feather Woman sat there shivering before she could move.

Sacred Bird gathered their few belongings and covered the fire with dirt to make sure it was out. She dismantled the little shelter and tried to make the place where they had slept as it was before. She scattered the little bushes they had used for the shelter.

She asked Sacred Feather Woman to join her in a little prayer before they started on their journey. They stood there and said their prayer for the journey to be a good one and to find Eagle Crier that day. After the prayer, Sacred Bird looked for any signs of tracks before they set out. She decided to look more closely for any tracks along the way. The sun was just beginning to come up over the horizon before they made their first rest stop. They ate a little before continuing.

Sacred Feather Woman wanted to rest, but Sacred Bird could not let her. She offered to carry her daughter on her back for a short distance. Sacred Bird endured the pain on her back and arms for as long as she could before she finally set her daughter down. She asked her daughter if she would walk until their next stop. They walked in silence for a while until they reached the top of a hill.

They stood at the top. Sacred Bird surveyed the distance, and just for a moment she thought she saw movement in the distance. She scanned the distant hill and saw what looked like horses. Her heart skipped a beat with gladness. 'That must be Eagle Crier and his family! We must be catching up with them at last!' she thought to herself before she told Sacred Feather Woman.

Sacred Bird looked down at Sacred Feather Woman and said, "I think Eagle Crier and his family are just ahead of us . . . just one hill away! We should get going and try to catch up before midday. Are you able to walk on your own now?"

Sacred Feather Woman looked up at her mother and smiled. "Yes, I could walk on my own . . . but who is Eagle Crier? Could we rest after we catch up with them?"

Sacred Bird nodded and said, "Yes, we will rest, and you will probably ride one of the horses so you don't have to walk so far. Eagle Crier has horses. He is a member of our people, and he is going home for a visit."

They started down the hill and quickened their pace. Sacred Bird was elated that they would finally have company and she would have someone to help her with her load. She knew if it was Eagle Crier and family, she and Sacred Feather Woman would be safe at night. Sacred Bird would not have to endure an ordeal as the night before. She looked forward to catching up with them.

Deep in her thoughts, Sacred Bird did not realize they had come upon a small creek. The creek was wide. "We will have to look for a crossing," she told Sacred Feather Woman.

The creek was deep in some places, but it was not as wide as a river. They went along the bank for a short distance before they found a large log by the creek.

Sacred Bird decided to throw the pouches to the other side so she could carry her daughter across. She placed the log as far across the creek as it would go and tested its security. She told her daughter that she would carry her. Sacred Bird instructed Sacred Feather Woman to hang on as she would not be able to hold her. She needed her arms to be free to balance herself as she walked across the log. If she had to, she would jump across from the end of the log to the edge on the other side.

She almost made it across. She was just about to jump when she lost her footing and they both fell in the freezing water. They emerged from the water soaking wet and muddy. Sacred Bird did not want to cry out loud, but she was in great pain from the fall. She had landed on something hard and head-first against the muddy bank.

After crawling from the water, they both laid on the bank trying to recuperate from the fall. Sacred Bird turned to look at her daughter to see if Sacred Feather Woman was ok; Sacred Feather Woman looked at her mother at the same time. They both burst out laughing as they pointed to each other. Sacred Feather Woman let out a squeal. Sacred Bird must have looked funny as she realized her face was black from the mud and her hair was stuck to her cheeks. Sacred Bird looked at her daughter and started laughing . . . Laughing felt good. It had been a long time since Sacred Bird laughed. She had forgotten how good it felt.

They changed their clothing after they washed the mud off their faces. They sat and talked about their little mishap before they continued their journey. They travelled at a good pace for most of the trek towards the other hill. Sacred Feather Woman walked, and then Sacred Bird carried her alternately. Sacred Bird wanted to catch up with Eagle Crier and his family. They reached the other hill not too long after their spill. The pouches were a little heavier from the wet clothing. For the first time since morning, Sacred Bird felt tired and wanted to find a resting spot.

Her body ached and her feet burned with pain, but she thought she should just keep going. As she looked to the south, she saw a hint of smoke off in the distance. 'That must be Eagle Crier's camp', she thought to herself.

She asked Sacred Feather Woman if she could walk on her own for a little while.

Sacred Feather Woman replied, "Why do you ask?"

Sacred Bird answered, "I just wondered if you could. I think we are catching up with Eagle Crier and his family. I think that they are camped just ahead. We could reach their camp in a short time, only if you can walk on your own, that way we can go a little faster."

She replied, "Let us go, then." Sacred Feather Woman reached down to pick up the pouch she had been carrying.

As they walked, Sacred Feather Woman asked questions about their journey, the whys and where they were going. Sacred Bird answered her questions and told her about their family back at the home camp. Sacred Bird even reminisced about the happier times back at the home camp. The memories of family all came flooding back in her mind and she could not help the tears as they rolled down her cheeks. Sacred Bird could not control her tears, and this alarmed Sacred Feather Woman.

Sacred Feather Woman reached up and took her mother's hand to console her. Sacred Bird sobbed as they walked. After the tears stopped, she looked at her daughter and told her that the tears were a mixture of loneliness and happiness, and that she did not fully understand them herself.

After many days of walking and camping alone, and after experiencing an incredible loneliness, they came upon a good rest area. As in previous days, Sacred Bird prepared the shelter and made the fire to warm them. Sacred Bird was developing a knack for making a shelter in no time. She had also developed a quick way to make a fire and was getting efficient in breaking camp and making it look like they were never there.

Then one day they reached Eagle Crier's camp just after midday. Eagle Crier was glad to see them. After the greetings, he told them he had camped to gather firewood and small game. Sacred Bird offered to help, but he told her to rest first. They sat around the fire exchanging news about their journey. Sacred Bird kept yawning, so he told her to rest. Sacred Bird and Sacred Feather Woman both fell asleep. It was close to sunset before they woke up.

Eagle Crier and his wife had made a shelter for themselves nearby in the small forest of alder trees. They made their shelter with sturdy branches to keep them warm and safe, especially for their young son. Eagle Crier suggested that Sacred Bird make a shelter next to theirs and he would help her. There were a few pine trees, but there were more white-barked trees. That night Sacred Bird and Sacred Feather Woman had a good night's rest, and they were kept warm by the robe that Eagle Crier's wife had let them use.

CHAPTER 7

JOURNEY WITH EAGLE CRIER AND FAMILY

That first morning with Eagle Crier and his family was pleasant. Sacred Bird looked forward to the journey ahead. She knew they would make it because the horses would carry the heavy load. Eagle Crier was well prepared. He had thought of all the necessities needed for a long journey. He was wise enough to conserve the dried food, which was lighter than fresh game.

His wife prepared the fresh game, a small animal, a small deer. Sacred Bird ate until she could not sit up. It has been a long time since she had a good meal. After the meal, Sacred Feather Woman played with the baby. Sacred Bird sat and relaxed that first day. Walks With Porcupine Woman was busy cooking the rest of the fresh meat and Eagle Crier was tending to the two travois that would carry the supplies and his family.

The next day, Sacred Bird helped with the preparations, alternately helping Eagle Crier and his wife while Sacred Feather Woman watched the baby. Sacred Bird was no stranger to hard work and was able to lift heavy items. On the other hand, Walks with Porcupine Woman was a delicate woman. Eagle Crier's wife was an attractive woman, small-framed with delicate features. Walks with Porcupine Woman was a gentle and kind woman. Her smile could make a bad day go the other way. She could speak some Blackfoot. She spoke softly and in a soothing voice.

That evening, they sat and talked of their families at the home camp. Eagle Crier came from the mountain clan, a clan Sacred Bird knew well. This clan usually camped near the mountains, and they were part of the nation Sacred Bird came from.

As they sat by the fire, Eagle Crier told stories of his grandfather's heroic feats and some funny stories to make them feel better. Laughing is medicine, which soothed their being and made life more bearable, even in the worst of times.

Both Sacred Bird and her daughter reluctantly retired for the night, and she did not want that brief happiness to end. Sacred Bird enjoyed the stories, especially the funny ones. They had laughed freely and temporarily forgot their journey ahead and the unpredictable weather the season brings forth sometimes. She had no trouble falling asleep for the first time since they left the northern camp. She felt at peace and her body welcomed the warmth of the heavy robe. She did not remember finishing her prayers.

Sacred Bird had such a good night's sleep that she awoke feeling well rested and raring to get on with the journey. Eagle Crier and his wife were already up and busy with their packing. Both glanced her way and told her to help herself to the food. Sacred Bird woke up Sacred Feather Woman. They ate, then together they packed their few belongings.

When the packing was done, Sacred Bird went to help the couple. Their baby had started crying and Sacred Bird's help gave Walks With Porcupine Woman the opportunity to tend to her baby's needs. Sacred Bird told the woman that she would be helping from now on so that the journey would be easier for all of them. Sacred Bird was eager to help wherever she was needed.

Sacred Bird worked in silence. Her thoughts turned to the journey ahead, and she wondered how long it would be. Her heart raced as she thought of her family at the home camp, and she could not wait to see their happy faces when she and Sacred Feather Woman finally got home. 'Oh, how the Elders will celebrate our return from what would be considered death,' she thought to herself. When her thoughts turn to loved ones, her heart raced and her body weakened, leaving her tired. She shook her head and decided to concentrate on the work and get on with the journey.

She turned to Eagle Crier and asked him, "Do you think the snow will come early . . . or do you think it will come just before we reach our destination?"

Eagle Crier stood and thought for a moment. He looked up at the sky before answering, "Yes, I think the time is closer when the snow will come . . . I have noticed the animals and the birds have been very busy preparing . . . why do you ask?"

Sacred Bird said, "I just thought maybe we could prepare ourselves by not staying too long on rest stops. You know how we get too comfortable . . . just like last night. I just don't want to be caught in a storm while we are still very far from our home camp."

"Yes, you are right; we will not waste too much time. We will travel as far as possible each day," said Eagle Crier as he went back to securing the load.

As he straightened up, Eagle Crier turned to Sacred Bird and asked, "Oh yes, I was going to ask you about some noises I heard last night, did you hear them? I know Walks With Porcupine Woman did not hear them, she was sound asleep."

Sacred Bird looked at Eagle Crier and replied, "No, I fell asleep before I could finish my prayers . . . what kind of noises did you hear?"

Eagle Crier said, "I can't quite describe them, but they seem to be coming from the north. I was just a little curious, but if you did not hear them, do not concern yourself with them. Maybe they are night animals hunting for their survival. Enough of them, let us get going, we have a long day ahead of us."

Sacred Bird went to Sacred Feather Woman and asked her if she was ready; Sacred Feather Woman said she was. Sacred Bird examined the pouches to make sure that everything was packed and made sure that their spare moccasins were in there. Eagle Crier asked Sacred Feather Woman if she wanted to ride one of the horses, but Sacred Feather Woman said she would like to walk until she got tired.

They put the fire out after everything was packed and arranged the area they had disturbed back to its original state as best they could before they started the journey. Eagle Crier called each of their names and told them to come along, that they are leaving this place and going home. The morning air was getting warmer, but it was still a bit cool. The cool mornings were a sign of the coming of another season and travelling kept them warm.

The surrounding plants were rapidly changing, as if to get ready for the new season which would come upon them soon. Even the sky was changing; the big fluffy clouds had been replaced by higher and greyer clouds. As Sacred Bird was taking in her surroundings, she heard the geese before she saw them. She pointed at them and told Sacred Feather Woman that the geese were leaving because of the new season coming. The days were getting shorter and cooler.

For most of the day, they travelled in silence, only the sounds of the horses' hooves on the almost frozen ground seemed to prod them to keep up with their pace. The horses would snort to break the silence. Walks with Porcupine Woman's baby would cry every now and then. Sacred Bird could hear Walks With Porcupine Woman's soothing voice singing a lullaby.

Sacred Bird was reminded of the baby she left behind. She wondered if she would ever see him again. She did not even give him a name, which made her sad. She knew that if she ever saw him again, she would know him because of his features. He also had a distinctive mark just above his belly button; it was this mark that truly connects him to her.

She felt the stinging pain of tears welling up in her eyes and knew that the scar of emptiness would never go away. She would carry this scar with her for the rest of her days and she would always feel the pain of emptiness in her arms for the child she never knew. She wiped the tears and hoped that the others did not notice them. Wiping the tears seemed to signal more tears to come. Sacred Bird had to stop and turn away from the others while she tried to control the tears. She prayed silently to the Creator. Praying seemed to help.

Sacred Feather Woman noticed that her mother had fallen behind and called out to her to ask if she was all right. Sacred Bird turned and told her she was fine, then quickened her pace to catch up with Sacred Feather Woman.

They stopped two times that day and ate. Eagle Crier looked up at the sky and told them that it would be clouding over tonight and said they would have to make their shelters a little more closed in for the cold night. There was plenty of daylight left, and he said it would be wise if they travelled a little more before they stopped for the day.

As they got to the top of a high hill, he pointed towards the next hill and said that he figured they would not reach it before sunset, but he said that they should be able to reach halfway up the hill. Sacred Bird looked and thought about the night in the trees. That hill had a little bit more trees than this last hill they had just climbed. She was not sure, but she felt a little uneasy about spending the night among so many trees, but she agreed that they should camp there.

They got to the site they had picked to camp for the night. Eagle Crier and his wife were busy making their shelter and not saying too much. While Sacred Bird and her daughter got busy gathering branches for their shelter, her thoughts turned to the dread she had felt earlier. She tried to make sense of the feeling and thought maybe this place had too many trees, but then she realized what she was dreading.

Sacred Bird knew that the noises would be paying her a visit again and she did not know if she should voice her fears to Eagle Crier. 'Maybe he won't believe me . . . or maybe he will believe me and tell me to leave', she thought to herself.

She had known what those noises were, and she knew where the spirits were from. Sacred Bird struggled with the knowledge and decided to pray about it before she told Eagle Crier about them. She also struggled with the information she would be sharing with Eagle Crier; he might banish them from travelling with him and his family.

They built their shelters on opposite sides of the fire. The firewood they had gathered for the night was piled next to each shelter. As they did each night, they sat and talked before going to sleep. Somehow that night was different. The laughter was missing, and they really did not talk about any specific subject, instead they struggled for the words.

Sacred Bird could not stand the awkwardness, so she told Eagle Crier and his wife about the night the spirits came to them. She did not leave any of the events of that frightful night out; she wanted to be truthful and honest about the incident.

Eagle Crier and his wife did not say anything. He seemed to contemplate and weigh the information Sacred Bird had just given them before he replied. He said that he knew what the noises were and did not want to alarm the group. He said that he knew right from the beginning that something like that would be happening because Sacred Bird would be the cause of it. Her relationship had much to do with it and it would not stop until the curse was lifted or beaten. Sacred Bird knew what he was talking about so she suggested maybe they should say their prayers together. Maybe the prayers would be stronger as a group.

That night, they said the prayers and Eagle Crier said that they should have discussed this before it got dark so they could have been better prepared. He said he knew what plant to use, so he would look for the plant the next day if it was not too late. Sacred Bird laid there most of the night wide awake and unable to fall asleep. She kept feeding the fire.

She heard all the noises that she had grown so accustomed to that night. There were no stars that night. When she looked up at the black sky, she saw forms. She would look at the fire and the same images would appear. There was no place to look. She sat up and shook her head. Her imagination must be over-active tonight, or was it her fears of what was to come taking over her being?

She fought with the forms for most of the night, closing her eyes and trying to pray, but no matter what she tried to do, the same forms were becoming more and more pronounced. The forms were moving in all directions, they seemed to dance in a taunting way, silently laughing at her.

She tried to focus her eyes on the shelter, but she could not see too well because of the forms. She could not call out to Eagle Crier and his wife. She hoped the forms were not real, that she was imagining them. She closed her eyes and tried to concentrate on her prayers, but it seemed as if her thoughts were irrational. Each prayer she started would lose itself in her head.

The forms were starting to take the shapes of terrifying beings, Sacred Bird could not stand it any longer and she cried out. Sacred Bird knew she was awake, but she could not seem to make her cries loud enough for the others to hear and then she was able to scream. The others finally woke up with her screams. Both Eagle Crier and his wife tried to calm Sacred Bird down. As they were trying to calm her down, they saw them. It seemed as if when the others saw them, the forms became real, and the sounds were so horrible that covering their ears did not seem to help. They could still hear them.

There were times, as the forms circled the little camp, that they seemed to come closer. Sacred Bird knew then that the forms were real to her; the stench of these creatures was so overwhelming. There was no way to escape the smell, and then the words became audible. Their words were cursing them, and she could hear her name being called, almost in a chanting way.

Eagle Crier and his wife and child were huddled together in prayer. Sacred Bird felt weak and tired. For the first time, she felt she should give up and save the others. Her whole body felt heavy. She could not move, and then the pains started. She remembered crying and screaming before losing consciousness.

The next thing she remembered was Sacred Feather Woman hovering over her, calling her, "Na'aa, Na'aa!" She was almost in tears.

Sacred Bird looked up. Her eyes felt as if they were full of sand, but she could see that Eagle Crier was burning Sweet Grass and murmuring his prayers. Sacred Bird tried to move but she was wrapped in the heavy robe. She tried to speak, but her mouth was so dry she could not say anything. Eagle Crier patted her head; Sacred Bird laid there and tried to form the words she wanted to say.

Walks With Porcupine Woman gently touched Sacred Bird's shoulder and said she should take a few drops of water first. She first wet Sacred Bird's lips with her fingertips and then she held the water skin to Sacred Bird's lips so that a few drops fell into her mouth. Those first few drops soothed Sacred Bird's parched mouth and she was able to speak. Just as Sacred Bird turned her head to ask questions, Eagle Crier told her not to speak yet.

Sacred Bird sat up with the help of Walks With Porcupine Woman and Sacred Feather Woman. She looked around and saw that it was almost daylight. The sky had greyer and darker clouds. She shivered and held the robe closer to her neck.

Walks With Porcupine Woman patted her head and said, "You are a strong woman." Sacred Bird didn't understand what Walks With Porcupine Woman meant.

Sacred Feather Woman sat beside her mother and gave her a hug and smile. Sacred Feather Woman looked so relieved that her mother was not harmed. Then Sacred Bird remembered the night. She took the robe off and took Sacred Feather Woman in her arms and told her daughter she was happy no one was harmed. They sat there for a while before Eagle Crier was ready to talk to Sacred Bird about the events of the night. Sacred Bird looked at him, trying to read his face.

He sat there and contemplated his words. After a while, he spoke. "Sacred Bird, I will tell you what I know, and I will tell you truthfully all that I know of the events. I have been living among Walks With Porcupine Woman's people for a few winters now and I have come to know who has medicine and how powerful their medicines are."

Eagle Crier continued, "Man With Many Medicines has many medicines. That is why he is called 'Man With Many Medicines'. He is a leader and has earned the respect of his people. His people have come to know the powerful medicines he possesses, and they look to him for cures and protection. He is not a person to fight with. Even though he has much to give and has shown his people that he is a sensitive and caring person, he can be quite the opposite if given sufficient cause."

He concluded, "Now, I am not putting the blame on you, but I want you to think about this and I will help you as much as I can. I have no medicines to stop such events from occurring again, but we must be very careful lest we are caught off guard. From now on, you must say your prayers with the Sweet Grass, and you must say your prayers four times a day. We will all do the same each day. I am not heartless to send you on your own. We will fight this together but remember, this is a curse put on you and there is no place to hide. Come, let us prepare for the day and be on our way."

That day, Sacred Bird's spirit was down. She tried to smile but no matter how much she tried, her smile felt like she was just showing her teeth. Sacred Feather Woman, too, looked so forlorn. Sacred Bird laboured in her mind to come up with a happy event she could relate to her daughter. She just could not find a happy or funny event. She finally resigned herself to sauntering along.

They stopped two times that day to pray and burn the Sweet Grass, and each time Sacred Bird felt a little better than before. The fourth time was before they retired for the night. She gave her whole being in prayer and had to believe that the previous night's events would not occur again. She had encouraged Sacred Feather Woman to do the same. Hearing her daughter's prayers made her feel better, and she knew she was not alone.

That night, even though she had prayed, she was still apprehensive. She concentrated on the Creator, who created all manner of life, even the medicine that was terrifying them. She was unable to fall asleep. Sacred Feather Woman was holding onto her hand. Sacred Bird noticed the others had no problem falling asleep. She chided herself for waiting up for the creatures and decided to try to sleep. She turned towards Sacred Feather Woman, her back to the fire.

Just as she felt comfortable, she heard the howling of wolves off in the distance. Their howling sounded as if there are many of them. She turned and got up to feed the fire, hoping to keep the surrounding area lit. As she lay there, the wolves' howling started to sound like they were coming closer. She sat up and decided not to sleep; she was going to be ready for them.

Sacred Bird sat up all night. Just before the morning light came, she saw the little men. They were scurrying in and out of the darkness, almost as if they were being mischievous. She closed her eyes and concentrated on praying. She was determined that the little men would not scare her. She knew there must have been a protective wall around the little camp, because the little men did not come close to the shelter.

She welcomed the morning and knew that this day would be good. She decided to gather some more firewood for the morning meal. She walked into the woods to find some dried twigs. She entered the woods somewhat noisily not too far from the small camp. Each step she took made noises because of the dried leaves and the old plants on the ground. As she bent down to pick up a few twigs, she heard what sounded like a growl ahead of her. It sounded as if it was coming from deep in the woods.

Sacred Bird felt a sudden rush of fear race through her body. Her heart raced and her mind told her to turn and run back to the camp, but her body would not respond. She stood frozen for a little while, then she remembered this feeling. This was the same feeling she had when she and Sacred Feather Woman got taken so long ago. This time she was able to move. She turned and ran as fast as she could. She ran as if it was right behind her.

She reached the camp, out of breath. Trying to catch her breath, she stood there and struggled to get the words out.

Eagle Crier and Walks With Porcupine Woman were just preparing to start the day. They had paused to listen to what Sacred Bird had to say, but Sacred Bird couldn't speak, she was still trying to catch her breath. They patiently waited for her to explain why she was running wildly back to the camp from the woods. They would look at her and then at the woods with a puzzled look.

Sacred Bird finally caught her breath and tried to explain that she had encountered a wild animal that had sounded huge, and she just wanted to warn them. All the while, Sacred Bird kept looking back at the woods to see if the animal would emerge.

Eagle Crier and Walks With Porcupine Woman both stood up and seemed genuinely alarmed at the information she was giving them. Then she heard it again. This time it was so close, as if it was right next to her. Sacred Bird stopped and both Eagle Crier and Walks With Porcupine Woman burst out laughing. Then Sacred Bird realized that it was her stomach telling her it was hungry! She felt so embarrassed and so foolish.

Sacred Bird sat down on the ground, relieved but embarrassed. Eagle Crier and his wife went over to her, and both patted her back.

Eagle Crier said, "Don't feel too bad, you are just on edge because of the events of the other night. This feeling of apprehension will pass. Before you know it, you will be yourself again. Don't let it take over most of your day."

CHAPTER 8

THE ARRIVAL OF WINTER

They finished the morning prayers and got busy, each with a specific chore to do before they resumed their journey. Sacred Bird was silent and tried to understand what she was going through. She had never been one to be so foolish and had always done her duties so meticulously and with as much accuracy as possible. But this time she had trouble tying a knot that would keep the bags closed. She did not have any energy to work fast.

Eagle Crier noticed and offered to help her. Normally Sacred Bird would thank him and say, 'no, I can do it,' but this time she let him tie the bags and load them on the travois. Sacred Feather Woman must have sensed something was wrong. In the past she had been very sensitive and caring and was always ready with a helping hand. She came and silently offered her hand to help her mother so they could start the journey.

Eagle Crier called out their names as he had done in the past, and they all started out. Sacred Bird sensed the change in the weather. There was a breeze coming from the north. This breeze seemed to tell her to beware. Its icy breath lingered to send a chill through to her bones. She walked along in a half-hearted pace, as if her legs were being forced to carry her. With each step, they protested.

She was silent most of the day while the others carried on as before, sharing stories and laughing and sometimes singing. Sacred Bird was aware of their happy noises, but for some reason she just could not take part. She tried to force herself to keep up with them, but she was content with being away from them. She could not understand herself. She felt a void inside her. 'What is it that is missing?' she wondered. Even thinking was a chore. Her feelings were numb. 'What is happening to me?' she thought to herself.

The next day was a blur. She had lost herself. She had not taken part in that portion of the journey. She had drifted along. Eagle Crier, Walks With Porcupine Woman, and Sacred Feather Woman each took turns to get her back to normal. Their attempts had failed that day or two, but their persistence paid off. She awoke one morning and was aware of her surroundings for the first time in what seemed a long time.

Sacred Feather Woman was awake when Sacred Bird woke up that morning. She sat up and reached over to touch her mother's cheeks. Sacred Bird opened her eyes, looked at her daughter, and smiled.

Sacred Feather Woman said, "Na'aa, you are back! You have come back to us." Sitting up, she called out to Eagle Crier. "Look . . . my mother has awakened!" Sacred Feather Woman turned to her mother with a big smile, her face radiant with happiness. She hugged her mother and said, "I am glad you are back." Sacred Feather Woman reached for her mother's hands and rubbed them on her cheeks.

Sacred Bird looked at her daughter and then at Eagle Crier with a look of not knowing what went on.

Eagle Crier sat up and smiled and nudged his wife to wake up. He said, "Sacred Bird, I am glad you are awake, you have had a long sleep; we have been very worried about you. We knew you would wake up because we have been praying for you. How do you feel?"

Sacred Bird replied, "I feel fine and well rested. How long have I been sleeping? I cannot remember when I fell asleep. I cannot believe I slept long. How did you manage with me as the extra burden?"

Eagle Crier held out his hand to stop Sacred Bird and said, "Wait, don't ask too many questions all at once." He smiled and added wood to the fire before he continued. "You fell behind and when we stopped, you did not catch up with us. It was then I decided to go back and see what was keeping you. I found you lying on the ground. I carried you for a little way and then I got the horse and used it to carry you. We tried to wake you, but you would not wake up. We knew you would come out of the sleep, but we did not know it would take almost two full days. The time that you slept, we prayed beside you and burned the Sweet Grass. I am thankful that you are awake. Your daughter cried some and we had a hard time trying to reassure her that you would be all right. She loves you and is lost without you."

Sacred Feather Woman was very happy that her mother was up and could not stop smiling and hugging her.

Sacred Feather Woman did not say too much. Walks With Porcupine Woman also came over and said she was pleased Sacred Bird was awake and hoped that she would be okay.

Eagle Crier cleared his throat and took the Sweet Grass from his bag and half-burned wood from the fire. He laid them out and said, "Come, gather around, let us pray." Turning to Walks With Porcupine Woman, he told her, "Take our son in your arms and we will all pray before we start the day."

They prayed, and for the first time in a few days, there was laughter and there was happiness in their voices. Sacred Bird was glad to be back and glad to be with this family. They prepared to leave after they ate.

Sacred Bird looked about and saw that there were very few trees, which seemed to be the reason for the colder wind. She shivered and pulled the small robe closed to fend off the biting wind. There was no snow yet, but the air felt cold; it would likely snow soon. The nearby trees were completely without their leaves and the ground had frost. She looked at the sky; the clouds seemed to be rushing south to warmer places.

She gathered the bags and helped with loading the belongings onto the travois. Eagle Crier was securing the loads while Walks With Porcupine Woman settled on the travois with her baby. Sacred Bird paused and looked at Walks With Porcupine Woman and her baby; they looked so snug and warm.

Walks With Porcupine Woman looked up at Sacred Bird and smiled and asked. "Are you going to be all right? You are not weak at all?"

Sacred Bird smiled and replied, "I will be okay, and I feel fine."

Sacred Bird looked and found a long stick to help her balance as she walked. As usual, Eagle Crier called each of them, telling them "It is time to go, time to go home."

Each of them started with a brisk walk, eager to shorten the distance between that place and the destination. The cold wind seemed to hasten their pace.

Sacred Bird looked around and tried to determine whether they were making progress. She could not recognize this part of the land. She was quite sure that Eagle Crier would know whether they were at least half-way to their destination. She hurried to catch up with Eagle Crier. He was leading the two horses.

Sacred Bird caught up with him and called out to him, "Eagle Crier, I want to ask you . . . how far do we have to travel yet? Do you know this part of the land? I thought I would be able to recognize this part of the land, but it seems the terrain is different."

Eagle Crier didn't slow his pace as he replied, "We are approaching the land where there are fewer trees. In fact, we are approaching a place where no man wants to live. It is bare of most of the plants, especially trees. The terrain is rough and sandy. We will not go through it, but we will bypass it and then we will have to cross a big river. We are more than half-way to our destination. We should reach our destination in good time if the weather is not too bad. You say you do not recognize this land? Maybe they took the easterly route."

Sacred Bird attempted to describe the land on the way north, as best as she could remember. Eagle Crier was not familiar with the land Sacred Bird had described.

They continued. As she thought about the terrain Eagle Crier had mentioned, Sacred Bird thought about the wood they would need if there were no trees on the way. She quickened her pace and caught up with Eagle Crier and again called out to him, "Eagle Crier, don't you think we should gather wood to bring along? I am worried that we might not be able to be warm if the snow comes. I don't want to freeze, and we should be prepared."

Eagle Crier looked at Sacred Bird and said, "Yes, you are right. At our next stop there will be plenty of trees and we will gather firewood for the journey. Do not worry too much. There will be some trees on the way."

Sacred Bird did not ask any more questions or question his knowledge about this part of the land. Their pace stayed the same and it became too much for Sacred Feather Woman. She agreed to ride on top of the provision travois. Eagle Crier made Sacred Feather Woman's ride as comfortable as possible and Sacred Feather Woman seemed content to ride.

Sacred Bird looked up at the sky. The clouds were getting greyer and the wind seemed a bit stronger than earlier. She had hoped that it would not snow yet, but the weather seemed a little ominous. They had been travelling for most of the day, stopping for a very short time to eat, rest, and pray. Sacred Bird noticed snowflakes flying about. She looked around and saw the clusters of trees ahead. She wondered if Eagle Crier would decide to camp there or move on. Just then, Eagle Crier slowed his pace and surveyed the surrounding land, seeming to look for a campsite.

She waited for him to tell them what he had decided. They approached the trees and then stopped. Eagle Crier walked around looking for a good place to camp for the night. Sacred Bird took the horses and held them to steady them; the horses seemed a little agitated. She called out to Sacred Feather Woman and asked if she was all right. Sacred Feather Woman replied and said she was warm. Sacred Bird called out to Walks With Porcupine Woman and she also replied she was ok.

Eagle Crier came back and said he found a good place to camp. He said there was a good shelter in the centre of the group of trees. There they camped for the night. The weather turned worse that night. Sacred Bird was thankful that Eagle Crier decided to pitch the small tepee for the night. Eagle Crier said it would be wise to stay in one tepee so that they could all keep warm for the night. If the weather let up a little the next day, they would be able continue the journey.

That evening, as they sat in front of the warm fire, they could hear the wind howling outside. Sacred Bird felt uneasy until after they said their prayers. They were all quiet as they sat and listened to the angry wind outside. They could hear the horses snort and move their hooves around to shift their weight. She hoped they would make it through this first cold snowy night.

Walks With Porcupine Woman broke the silence and told them she was going to sleep. She said she did not feel well. She and Eagle Crier spoke in low tones and then Eagle

Crier turned to Sacred Bird and asked if she could stay up for a while and feed the fire. Sacred Bird told him she would be happy to stay up and make sure the tepee was warm.

Sacred Bird turned to Sacred Feather Woman and asked if she felt tired. Sacred Feather Woman said she was tired and would like to go to sleep. Sacred Bird made sure her daughter was nice and warm before going to sleep. Sacred Bird bound her daughter's feet, ankles, and legs with the strips of hide to keep her feet and legs warm.

The next day, the snow and wind eased up a bit and they were able to continue with the journey. Sacred Bird noticed that Walks With Porcupine Woman and her baby were unusually quiet, but then she rationalized that maybe they were too comfortable. Sacred Bird was quiet for most of the day. The only time she spoke was to ask Sacred Feather Woman if she was warm and comfortable, and each time her daughter would reply she was.

They reached a group of trees just before it became dark. This time Walks With Porcupine Woman did not help, so it took Sacred Bird and Eagle Crier a little longer to put the tepee up. They got the tepee up just before the next onslaught of snow and wind.

Sacred Bird asked Eagle Crier if his wife and baby were going to be all right. He looked at Sacred Bird with a worried voice. He said he was not happy about their health. Both were burning up with fever and this last move was a bad one. He said he regretted this last move and should have stayed at the last place they camped at. There were more trees and the shelter from the snow and wind was better.

Sacred Bird tried to reassure him that maybe he should not be too hard on himself and that she will help him. That evening, Walks With Porcupine Woman and her baby took a turn for the worse. Eagle Crier could only pray. It upset him very much not being a medicine man and not knowing what to do.

Sacred Bird stood by helplessly. The only thing she could do was make sure there was enough firewood. She spent so much time gathering twigs and big branches from the trees outside in the storm that she was exhausted by the time she finished. The cold was taking its toll on them all and she became worried.

Sacred Bird sat down. With her hands she covered her face, bowed, and prayed a silent prayer. Somehow she knew something was going to happen, but she could not quite figure out what was about to happen or how she knew what was about to happen. She could not discuss anything with Eagle Crier because he had his own worries and Sacred Feather Woman was sleeping. She decided to go out and get more wood for the fire. She fed the fire before she went out.

Once outside, she had to fight the wind to get to the trees. The struggle to get firewood in a storm is never easy, and this time the wind seemed to burn her skin and she could not be choosy anymore. She grabbed dead branches and twigs from the trees and if they did not break off, she moved onto the next tree. Each time she went out she came back with less wood, and each time she went out she had to go farther to get the few.

Sacred Bird spent most of the night running in and out of the small tepee. The running exhausted her. Her hands were feeling numb, so she decided to thaw them before she went out again. The type of wood she was bringing in did not burn as easily as the dried ones, and the wood made more smoke than heat. She had to cover Sacred Feather Woman's mouth so her daughter would not breathe the smoke in her sleep. She also had to make sure that Eagle Crier and his family did not inhale the smoke while sleeping.

The last time she ran out to get more wood, she thought she saw some creatures that looked like tiny animals or men. They were only as tall as the height of her knees, and she did not have a good look at them. They scurried out of sight before she could get a good look at them. She thought she was seeing things and that her mind was being affected by the cold wind and snow, which blew hard and seemed to bite into her skin and blind her eyes. She was a little annoyed with herself for being so clumsy, tripping over every little obstacle in her path. At times she almost fell on them. She tried to convince herself that these creatures did not exist and the noises they made were inaudible, that the noises were made by the wind and snow.

It was only after she went inside that she felt alarmed. She felt a tingling sensation on the back of her neck, and she dreaded to go out again. She knew she was not a very brave person and she decided to wake Eagle Crier if the creatures came inside. The fire did not die down completely when morning came, however it was cold inside the tepee and Sacred Bird had added the last of the wood to the fire before she fell asleep.

She woke up to the mournful cries of Eagle Crier and his wife. Sacred Bird sat up and looked over to Eagle Crier;

he was rocking back and forth. She felt weak with fear and then panic. Her heart skipped a beat, seeming to beat very irregularly, and then she had to gasp before she tried to say something. She had a hard time getting the words out. She crawled and was half-way over to Eagle Crier and his wife before she could say anything.

Sacred Bird asked, "What is wrong?" And when she reached them, she saw the lifeless body of Eagle Crier's baby in his arms.

Walks With Porcupine Woman was sitting up and sobbing uncontrollably. She had no words and started to cry too.

That morning, they took the baby's body and wrapped it in a robe and laid it to rest on a tree branch not far from the tepee. Both parents were devastated and inconsolable. Sacred Bird could not find the words to comfort them.

For the first time, she knew that this tragedy was a victory for the man she had left. She knew he was not going to stop until he accomplished what he set out to do. He was going to prevent Sacred Bird from reaching her destination, and in the process he would do whatever it took to make her suffer by hurting those close to her.

Sacred Bird's heart sank as she realized that she had no power to go against this man. She did not even begin to know the first thing about fighting back. She did not even have visions or dreams that she could use. She must instead rely on her own common sense and most of all on the Creator.

Throughout that morning, everyone was quietly mourning the baby, each with their own thoughts. The next few days were like that. Sacred Bird was the only one up and about. She could not sit still; she had to be busy. She gathered wood for the fire and tried to feed everyone, but Eagle Crier and his wife only ate a little. They did not seem to want to do anything, they sat and held each other and cried until they went to sleep.

Sacred Feather Woman was quiet as she rested for most of the day. She had her arms under her head and just stared, almost blankly. Sacred Bird could see the pain and pity on her face. For the first time in a few days, Sacred Bird felt a lump in her throat and felt so helpless. She sat there feeling weak and vulnerable. Part of her wanted to run outside and gather wood and part of her wanted to mourn with the others and give up!

She finally got up and went outside and tripped just as she closed the flap, but she held out her hands and landed on all fours in the snow. She hesitated and got up. Her hands were stinging with pain from the cold snow. She quickly brushed the snow off by using her robe.

The wind and snow pounded mercilessly against her face as she headed toward the trees. She grabbed as many twigs and branches as she could before she headed back to the tepee. Her ears, nose, and chin felt just as numb as her legs and hands. The cold and snow made her forehead numb.

Just as she was about to enter the tepee, she looked over to the horses. Both were still standing in the same position as before. She entered the tepee and noticed everyone had not altered their positions, just as the horses had not, and this disturbed her. She fed the fire, her mind heavy with thoughts about a way out of here. 'If only the wind and snow would stop and give us a chance to prepare to leave this place,' she thought to herself.

Sacred Bird sat down next to Sacred Feather Woman and brushed her daughter's hair away from her eyes. Sacred Feather Woman had closed her eyes to sleep. Sacred Bird looked over to Eagle Crier and his wife, both were still sitting and holding each other, their eyes closed as if they were sleeping. Sacred Bird sat there for a long time while everyone slept. She pondered their plight and decided to tell Eagle Crier that they must leave with the first light of dawn if the weather let up a bit.

Sacred Bird looked at their provisions, the food was dwindling. The amount of food did not look like there would be enough to feed all of them; there might be enough for a day. She sat and stared at the dried meat. Her heart sank as she realized that the wind and snow might not let up for a few days.

Sacred Bird sat there trying to think of a way to get everyone to come back from this 'giving up' situation. She sat there and thought of different ways of telling the others, but she could not think of a way to tell them, other than just to say what was on her mind. She thought she must encourage them if they were to survive.

CHAPTER 9

THE CRUEL WINTER

The days spent at the camp where Eagle Crier's baby died felt like many, many moons. Sacred Bird had discovered why the horses stood in the same position for so long. They had frozen to death. The loss of the baby and the horses was devasting to the group, and to make matters worse, their food and choice firewood supplies were also getting low.

Sacred Bird was worried. She told Eagle Crier that since the horses were dead, they might as well use them as food. Eagle Crier did not say anything. Sacred Bird began to cut pieces of meat from the horses to keep everyone from starving. Finding good firewood was difficult. The dead branches that burn easily were quite high on the trees or were buried in the snow. She would chip pieces from the bottom of the tepee poles to keep the fire going and to keep everyone warm.

Sacred Bird called Eagle Crier and his wife to get their attention. She carefully chose her words to comfort and urge them to be strong. She knew if they stayed, the poles would be considerably shorter and the wood she was getting from underneath the snow did not burn easily. She was also worried that chipping away at the tepee poles would compromise the shelter of the tepee.

Eagle Crier and his wife sat there for a long time listening to Sacred Bird. When Sacred Bird had finished her talk of encouragement, she asked Eagle Crier to pray and burn the Sweet Grass. He reluctantly took his bag to prepare for the prayers. His wife did not move, so Sacred Bird gently patted Walks With Porcupine Woman's shoulder and urged her to help her husband. Walks With Porcupine Woman moved closer to her husband.

Sacred Bird also asked Sacred Feather Woman to join in the prayers. Eagle Crier started the prayers. The prayers seemed to help a little and got everyone interested in keeping warm. They gathered around the fire to warm themselves and then they asked for food. This got Sacred Bird's spirits up and she was glad to venture outside into the cold to get more meat. She managed to get some wood covered by the snow and chip some from the bottom of the tepee poles to cook the meat.

Eagle Crier talked for a while after they ate. He told them that they must prepare to leave this place with the first light of day in the morning. Sacred Bird was glad he was almost back to normal. She knew he was still hurting from his loss. She could see the pain in both of their faces. Walks With Porcupine Woman looked older from the pain. Her delicate features were clouded in the pain of her loss and the pain of her sickness. Sacred Bird could not find the comforting words and could only manage to pat Walks With Porcupine Woman's shoulders and smile reassuringly.

That next morning, the wind and snow let up a bit. They managed to prepare as best as they could for the harsh journey ahead. Each of them wore everything that they had and carried what they could. Eagle Crier did not call out their names this time, so this time Sacred Bird called out each of their names. It felt strange calling out the names because the mood was heavy with the grief over the death of the baby. Walks With Porcupine Woman looked like she was lost. Walks With Porcupine Woman stood for a while and only moved when Eagle Crier took her arm and led her.

Everyone was silent that day. They had travelled a long way even though the snow was a hindrance. They stopped to rest underneath some thick bushes on the way and ate a little of the meat Sacred Bird was carrying. They did not make a fire. Eagle Crier broke the silence by telling them that they should be near a big river and that they would camp on the other side. He reassured them that they should be warm for the night and there should be some trees. He said they would be able to make a shelter there. No one said anything, they were all tired from the loads and the walk, which was made difficult by the snow and terrain.

The snow was deep in some parts, and it made everyone a little clumsy. Sacred Bird tried her best to keep her balance, but it was hard. She was holding Sacred Feather Woman to prevent her from falling. It was cold and the wind had not let up. She was thankful the snow was not blowing in their faces, but still the wind bit into their skin like little knives and they had to walk hunched over to protect their skin from freezing.

Eagle Crier was not so fortunate; he was having problems keeping Walks With Porcupine Woman on her feet. She seemed as if she had lost all sense of balance, and this took a toll on Eagle Crier. They would fall or trip and Sacred Bird would help them as best as she could. Eagle Crier and his wife always managed to get up and keep going.

Sacred Bird did not know how long they had travelled or how far they had travelled but the day was ending, and the wind was increasing its wrath. Her arms were aching with the weight of the load; the load seemed to get heavier with each step she took. She finally called out to Eagle Crier. "Eagle Crier . . ." she was almost out of breath. "Let us stop . . . let us adjust the loads . . . we should try to unload whatever we don't need . . ." Sacred Bird gasped for breath. Her mouth felt dry and it was hard for her to talk with her mouth almost frozen.

Eagle Crier and his wife caught up with them. They were not far behind Sacred Bird and Sacred Feather Woman, only a few steps, but they took some time catch up.

Eagle Crier was also gasping for breath. When he was able to speak, he said, "We cannot stop here . . . it is too dangerous here . . . let's try to make it to that group of trees ahead . . ." He pointed to a small group of trees and bushes.

"Yes," Sacred Bird replied as she bent down to encourage Sacred Feather Woman to try her best to walk a little farther. She reassured her that they would make a warm fire there.

Sacred Bird straightened and tried to smile at Walks With Porcupine Woman, but her mouth seemed as if it would crack. Walks With Porcupine Woman had her face covered with the robe that kept her warm. She did not have to carry anything. Eagle Crier and Sacred Bird agreed it would be best if his wife did not carry a load, they did not want her to get too sick.

They reached the little cluster of trees just as it got dark. Eagle Crier and Sacred Bird decided a fire should be made before they started on the shelter. They gathered the firewood. The little bushes had a lot of firewood to offer, there were so many dead branches. Sacred Bird was thankful for that and did not stop gathering when Eagle Crier told her to stop. He had to yell at Sacred Bird and that brought her back to her senses.

She stopped and looked at him; he was standing by the bushes and holding onto a tall tree. The tree did not have a big trunk, it was slender. When Sacred Bird looked closely, it was a berry bush, but it was sturdy enough to hold the little tepee up.

She walked over and started helping him with the shelter, while Sacred Feather Woman and Walks With Porcupine Woman huddled near the fire to keep warm. Both had very bad coughs. It seemed as if they were taking turns coughing. Putting up the tepee was very difficult, and it was dark by the time they finished.

When the tepee was up, they started cutting small branches to use underneath the robes they used as beds. The small branches would help keep them warm. Next, they built a small fire in the middle of the makeshift tepee.

Once finished, the tepee was warm, and everyone settled in for the night. They talked only when they had to. There was no happiness in the air, but at least they were warm. Sacred Feather Woman and Walks with Porcupine Woman both rested after they ate some of the meat Sacred Bird had taken along.

Eagle Crier tended to his wife and made her as comfortable as possible. His face looked tired and worn from the cold and from the worry.

Sacred Bird looked at him and asked, "How is she?"

He did not reply, he just looked at Sacred Bird and shook his head slightly. Sacred Bird felt alarmed and helpless. Her only thought was, 'This can't be, we have been plagued with bad incidents and I don't know what to do!'

Sacred Bird made Sacred Feather Woman as comfortable as possible and even sang a lullaby to help her sleep. After Sacred Feather Woman fell asleep, Sacred Bird crawled over to where Walks With Porcupine Woman was and felt her forehead. She was burning up with fever and her breathing was not good. She looked at Eagle Crier and suggested he should burn the Sweet Grass and pray. Sacred Bird did not know what else to do.

That night, the wolves howled and kept Sacred Bird awake all night. They sounded as if they were just outside the entrance to the tepee. She was thankful there was enough firewood. She was also thankful Eagle Crier was awake most of the night. It was almost morning when Sacred Bird finally fell asleep.

The noise of the wind woke her up and she sat up, listening with dismay. She looked at Sacred Feather Woman; her daughter was still sleeping. As always, she brushed her hair away from her face. Sacred Bird felt her daughter's forehead;

Sacred Feather Woman was feverish. She looked over to Eagle Crier and his wife, they were still sleeping.

Sacred Bird got up and added more wood to the fire and searched the bags for food. There was only a little bit of the meat left. She waited until the fire went well before she warmed the meat over the open fire. After the meat was warmed, she divided it into four. She hoped that the meat would help nourish and strengthen Sacred Feather Woman and Walks With Porcupine Woman. After a while, everyone stirred and got up. Sacred Bird told them that the meal was ready.

Eagle Crier and Sacred Bird ate their portions but Sacred Feather Woman and Walks With Porcupine Woman could not eat. They tried, but they could not eat. Sacred Bird saw how they struggled, so she suggested they save their food in case they got hungry later.

Eagle Crier spoke after he finished his meal, "Have you gone out to see how the weather is? It sounds like the wind is picking up and another storm is going to hit us again."

Sacred Bird replied, "No, I haven't gone out, but I will find out . . . I have to get more firewood." She reached for her robe and moccasins and went out into the cold. She walked over to the pile of firewood she had stacked from the night before. As she was walking, she noticed the tracks. The tracks seemed to be all over. She tried to determine what made the tracks, but the wind had blown some snow into them, and it was hard to tell what made them. They were bigger than her fist. She wondered if the tracks were made by the wolves they heard the night before.

She went back inside the small tepee. She told Eagle Crier, "It is colder today than yesterday, and I do not think it is wise to continue the journey with both Sacred Feather Woman and Walks With Porcupine Woman not feeling well."

Eagle Crier replied, "Yes, you are right. I was going to suggest that we stay here for a few days until Sacred Feather Woman and Walks With Porcupine Woman are better. I do not want to risk getting them too sick, we should wait until they are a little better, or when the weather is a little more agreeable."

They stayed at that place for many days. Sacred Bird would remember those days they spent together. The storm hit them one day after the wind blew from the north. Sacred Bird had gathered enough firewood to last for a few days and she had piled them inside the tepee. She lined the wall with them. She did this to protect them from the wolves; the wolves frequently came during the nights.

She had been up one night when one came sniffing at the entrance. She had a very heavy stick in her hand that she used to hit the wolf with. She did not know if she injured the wolf, but the wolf ran away yelping. This did not deter the others, a few came to the entrance and each time Sacred Bird slammed the stick against the tepee, which shook the shelter.

Finally, Eagle Crier said something. Sacred Bird thought he was sleeping. Without getting up or even lifting his head, he just said, "Don't hit the tepee too hard, you will knock it down and then we will be out in the cold."

After that Sacred Bird would just tap lightly whenever a wolf came to the entrance. She was getting frightened. The wolves were coming to the entrance more frequently and she was determined that they were not going to come in and disrupt them and this little tepee. She was spending the nights making sure the wolves stayed away and making sure that the others had their rest. She slept during the day and gathered the firewood just before dark.

One day Eagle Crier went out to search for food and he came back with a porcupine. The porcupine did not look too appetizing with its quills and straight hair sticking up from its back. They all joked about the food. Even Sacred Feather Woman and Walks With Porcupine Woman enjoyed themselves teasing Eagle Crier. Sacred Bird enjoyed seeing and hearing them, their faces happy and almost healthy, as they joked and teased Eagle Crier.

It was Walks With Porcupine Woman who said that she should change her name after the meal. She said, "After this, I will be known as the woman who no longer walks with the porcupine, but the woman who ate the porcupine who walked with her."

They had such a good time laughing and talking well into the evening. The meat was not bad. It would at least keep them from starving.

The next few days were uneventful. Both Sacred Feather Woman and Walks With Porcupine Woman were getting better. The time to leave this place was near. The rest of the journey was going to be all right. Sacred Bird looked forward to the next part of the journey. She knew that Sacred Feather

Woman and Walks With Porcupine Woman were going to be well enough, so hopefully the journey would be pleasant.

She recalled the happier times they had shared earlier. She had no idea this journey would have so much happen. She had not expected that this journey would be plagued with misery.

They had managed to survive on porcupine and rabbit. Sacred Feather Woman and Sacred Bird still could not get used to eating rabbit. They had never tasted rabbit until they came to the northern camp. They had no choice but to eat, otherwise they would have gone hungry.

Eagle Crier said that catching the porcupine was easy; all he had to do was swat it off a tree. The other way was to strike the porcupine on the head with a blunt object, and he emphasized the need to avoid the quills located on the tail. Catching the rabbit was a different matter. Eagle Crier described his efforts to catch the rabbit.

With his hands, Eagle Crier motioned how he managed to stun the rabbit with a stick. He had intended to snare the rabbit with a rope but somehow it slipped through, and Eagle Crier desperately wanted to catch the rabbit, so he threw a long stick after it. Eagle Crier said he was surprised he hit the rabbit and when he tried to pick it up by the ears, the rabbit came to. Eagle Crier said he did not have time to think, he instinctively threw the rabbit, slamming it against a tree and breaking its neck.

One night they sat and conversed for a while before they turned in for the night. Sacred Bird had been trying to sleep during the night at the insistence of Eagle Crier. Eagle Crier explained that she would need to be awake during the day for the next part of the journey. He reassured her that he would keep watch on them all throughout the night and that Sacred Bird should not worry about the wolves.

They planned their journey. Eagle Crier said the next part of the journey should not be more than a few days, if the weather held out. However, he said that if the weather was cold, it should be in their favour. There were rivers to cross, and the river would be frozen and should be sturdy enough to hold their weight. They all decided what they could carry and how they would carry the small amount of food.

Eagle Crier said that they must carry a bundle of the firewood. He was not sure there would be enough firewood on this next part of the journey. He said he recalled that there might be fewer trees on part of the journey, but he was not sure, so just to be on the safe side they should have some with them in case they needed to warm themselves.

They travelled quite far that first day, stopping three times before they decided to camp for the night. They had come upon a little valley. They searched for a suitable spot for the camp and finally found one. They decided to make the tepee against the side of a small dirt cliff with a tall rock not far from a small creek. There were a few trees, not very big trees, and they stood far apart from each other.

They decided to make the shelter by the rock. Eagle Crier said that the rock would offer protection from any animals that might roam by. So Eagle Crier and Sacred Bird set out to get what was needed to set up the tepee, or half a tepee. Eagle Crier made a fire for his wife and Sacred Feather Woman to warm themselves. Then both Eagle Crier and Sacred Bird had a discussion on how they should set up the tepee.

It was difficult to make the tepee stay up by the rock. They finally came up with a solution. They decided to add more rawhide rope length to the top side of the tepee and tie it down on one side of the rock. The rock was not very big, but it was quite tall. They had a difficult time, but they finally had to cut a small tree and use it to keep the tepee up.

The tepee was not as warm as they had anticipated. They were cold that night. They could not keep the fire going all night because the wood was not dry enough and the fire was too near the entrance. The next morning, they managed to cook the meat and prepare for the trek in the cold.

They decided to use the strips of hide to wrap their feet and legs as protection from the icy wind. The clouds were dark and heavy with snow and seemed to be getting ready to let go of their load. Sacred Bird's thoughts turned to her loved ones at the home camp in the south. She wondered what they would be doing and where they would be camping. As always, her heart raced with anticipation at seeing them. She then realized that she had been gone for two winters. She wondered how tall her sons would be.

They had travelled for most of the day when Sacred Bird wondered if Eagle Crier had called out their names for the journey. She stopped and tried to remember whether he did. She turned to Eagle Crier and asked him, "Eagle Crier, did you call out our names before we started this morning?"

Eagle Crier stopped in his tracks and answered, "No, I don't know if I did. I don't think I did . . . I should have been reminded. I'm sorry, I have made a mistake." He looked up at the sky as though he was talking to someone up there and said, "Let us stand here and call our names . . . maybe it will help."

So they stood there in the cold and took turns calling each other.

CHAPTER 10

HARDSHIPS

A few days of travelling in the cold and with little rest took a toll on them. They finally reached the river that Eagle Crier had talked about. Sacred Bird was very tired. For the first time since she had that episode of not remembering, she felt drained. The weakness she felt at that time returned and she could not help as before.

Her legs felt weak, and her knees could not take the strain and would crumple, which made the crossing difficult. She slipped and fell almost on Sacred Feather Woman several times as they walked across the river. Sacred Bird warned her daughter. Sacred Feather Woman did not heed her warning. Sacred Feather Woman wanted to help her mother and Sacred Bird narrowly missed her daughter each time she fell.

Eagle Crier attempted to help Sacred Bird, but he had his hands full with Walks With Porcupine Woman, who was also weak and needed his help more to keep her balance. They almost lost their balance a few times, and those few times their loads fell and filled with snow. Sacred Bird was covered with snow by the time they reached the other side of the river. The load she carried had fallen apart from the falls. Sacred Bird made feeble attempts to brush the snow off before she got too cold.

When they got to the other side they were so cold, they were all shivering. Sacred Bird sat there trying to regain what little strength she still had before she could be of any use. Eagle Crier walked toward the trees looking for a site for the camp. Walks With Porcupine Woman was also sitting down. Sacred Feather Woman wandered off to the trees to explore this place. Sacred Bird groaned every time she moved.

Eagle Crier returned and said, "I found a perfect spot for the camp and there is plenty of firewood to keep warm for the night. Come and help me set up the camp." He spoke to no one in particular. Walks With Porcupine Woman and Sacred Bird looked at each other without saying a word, neither of them making a move.

After a short while, Sacred Bird got up slowly and went to help Eagle Crier. Walks With Porcupine Woman made a gallant effort to come to their aid but was of little use. Eagle Crier's wife seemed to be weaker than before. Sacred Bird finally suggested that Walks With Porcupine Woman sit and rest. It was better that she rested.

Eagle Crier expressed his fear of crossing the river as an attempt to make conversation as they proceeded to work. He said, "I was afraid that the ice on the river might be too thin for us. I was going to tell you that maybe we should not walk too close together . . . our combined weight might be too much for the ice . . . but I'm glad we made it across without falling through."

Sacred Bird did not say anything, she just nodded. She was too tired and cold to say anything.

It was late, but the sun had not set. They finished putting up the tepee, a little floppy, but it would keep them warm for the night. As they sat in the tepee with the fire going, they heard the wolves howling and an owl hooting somewhere in the trees. The wolves and the owl sounded so near that Sacred Feather Woman was afraid and moved closer to her mother for safety. Sacred Bird, on the other hand, was too tired to be affected by the fierceness of the howls. She just sat, numb from the tiredness she felt. She reached out and held her daughter until Sacred Feather Woman felt safe enough to lie down and rest.

Walks With Porcupine Woman, for the first time in a long time, somehow found the strength to get busy with preparing the meat for the meal. Sacred Bird heard Walks With Porcupine Woman tell Eagle Crier that he would have to find some food soon. Sacred Bird drifted off to sleep. She slept through the night. She did not have the energy to eat before she went to sleep.

The next morning, she woke up still a bit tired and hungry. She decided to venture out into the cold. She got ready, wrapped her feet and legs, fed the fire, and went out.

It was almost daylight. She looked up at the cloudy sky. It was calm and she thought this would be a perfect day to travel. She scanned the surroundings. There were tall trees on this side and short bushes. As she turned, she noticed the hill sloping away from the trees. The hill was not steep, and it would not take too much energy to climb it. She wondered what the land would be like. She wondered if she should climb the hill and see for herself. After a few moments, she decided to wait until they started the journey.

Sacred Bird walked around taking in the white and blue scenery and examining the fresh tracks that were in the snow not far from the shelter. As she looked closely, she heard what sounded like a big cat. She was not quite sure where the roar came from. She stood and listened. When she heard it again, it seemed to be coming from across the river.

She decided she would inform the others. She returned to the tepee and found them still sleeping. She added more wood to the fire. Just then the others stirred, and after a while they got up after she had cooked the meat.

Eagle Crier spoke first and asked if it was still early yet. Sacred Bird replied, "Yes, it is still early. We still have time to prepare for the journey . . . this is a good day to travel . . . I just came back . . . but just before I returned, I saw fresh tracks in the snow and as I was looking at them, I heard a roar . . . it sounded like a big cat."

This caught Eagle Crier's attention; he looked at Sacred Bird and asked if she saw the big cat. Sacred Bird replied, "No, I didn't . . . but I am certain that it is, I have heard that roar before in the mountains."

Eagle Crier said that they must be careful, and then he went outside to investigate.

Sacred Feather Woman asked, "Na'aa, will this animal attack us?"

Sacred Bird replied, "No. If we head away from it and its food, it will not bother us."

Walks With Porcupine Woman listened as Sacred Bird and her daughter spoke about the big cat, and she too expressed her fear of animals such as the big cat.

Eagle Crier returned and said, "I don't trust this weather . . . it is unsettling . . . I hope it's like this throughout the day . . . are you afraid to go on?"

No one answered, as if all were weighing the question that was just asked.

Sacred Bird was the first to speak, "I'm not afraid, but if you are . . . then we should wait. I do not know how the weather is in this part of the land. It is up to you. What do you think?"

Eagle Crier replied, "We must proceed with caution and be well prepared. I know this part of the land, sometimes a blizzard will come without warning, and it usually comes when you least expect it. I have seen it happen once before. I was lucky I was with my friends and they knew what to do."

"What did you do when the blizzard came?" Sacred Bird asked.

Eagle Crier went on to explain, "At that time, we were caught in the open prairie and there was no shelter. There were no trees, so we just dug ourselves in the snow drift and huddled together to keep warm under the snow. We could not build a fire. There was no wood and we did not have a tepee. That was when we were young and foolish and had wandered off far from the home camp."

This little bit of information gave Sacred Bird hope that they must be near their destination. She suggested that they prepare for the journey home. She was excited to see her family again.

They prepared to start the journey. The climb to the top of the hill took a little time, there were places where the drifts were deep which made the climb difficult. They encountered little bushes that caught the wrappings on their feet and legs. They would stop and fix the wrappings. Once they reached the top, Sacred Bird could see far. She tried to determine whether she could recognize the landmarks ahead.

As she looked to the west, she saw the faint outline of what looked like the mountains. She was elated to see them. Some were behind the clouds.

She stood there and stared, trying to convince herself that those were the mountains! She turned to Eagle Crier and asked him. He said they were. She asked him if he knew how far they had yet to travel. He replied that it should take them a few more days. He said, "If we had horses, it would take us less time."

This made Sacred Bird happy, and her energy was renewed. She felt as if she was walking with a bounce. The spring in her step was contagious, both Sacred Feather Woman and Walks With Porcupine Woman also looked happy. They all showed their happiness in their walk and on their faces.

They travelled quite far that day. Eagle Crier pointed out some landmarks that he recognized in the distance. They could not make out what they were, the landmarks were too far and all they saw were the dark blue outlines of the hills he was pointing at. No one argued with him. They simply agreed that they did see the landmarks.

It was late in the day when they all agreed that they had travelled far enough and should set up camp for the night. They managed to find some tall bushes to camp by. Setting up the small tepee took little time. After they had built a fire, they settled in for the night. They were all so exhausted, they only ate a little.

That night, Sacred Bird was awakened by strange noises, like a chant, coming from the north side of the shelter, but at a distance. She did not say anything. She thought she was the only one hearing the chants. Eagle Crier startled her when he nudged her on the shoulder. She almost cried out. He silently motioned that he heard the noises. Sacred Bird nodded and turned to Sacred Feather Woman to wake her.

Sacred Bird turned to Eagle Crier and his wife. They were both sitting up. They all sat and listened for a short while. Eagle Crier reached into his bag and pulled out the Sweet Grass. When Sacred Bird saw that the Sweet Grass was just about gone, she felt alarmed. The expression on Eagle Crier's face told her that he too knew the consequences of not having any Sweet Grass.

No one made a sound until the fragrance of the Sweet Grass filled the tiny tepee. Sacred Bird whispered to Sacred Feather Woman that she too must say her prayers. They had a terrible time fighting the evil spirits throughout that night. They did not have a good night's rest. They sat huddled together all night.

Sacred Bird was the one being attacked. She remembered screaming for a time until she came partially to her senses.

Walks With Porcupine Woman and Sacred Feather Woman prayed while Eagle Crier burned the Sweet Grass. Sacred Bird was not sure how many times Eagle Crier burned the Sweet Grass that night.

Sacred Bird was afraid to see something that represented the noises, so she closed her eyes, but it was hard for her to keep them closed. She had to protect Sacred Feather Woman by holding her and shielding her from whatever was terrorizing them. She had chills and stomach pains. The pains were so uncomfortable. No matter which way she turned, the evil spirits were there circling the little shelter. She was so involved in her own battle and was not aware of Eagle Crier and his wife's struggles. Sacred Feather Woman was so terrified that she shook and could not stop shivering.

The next morning, Sacred Bird was so exhausted that she fell asleep, and it seemed as if she had just closed her eyes to sleep when she felt someone tapping her shoulder. She looked up and it was Eagle Crier. He had this strange expression that Sacred Bird could not figure out. He was incoherent at first. Sacred Bird got up and tried to under-stand what it was Eagle Crier was trying to say.

The spirits left before dawn. All was quiet. They sat for a while, exhausted from a night of terror. Eagle Crier spoke up and said, "I am very afraid, and the medicine that has been shot at us has been increasing in power. We must be on guard from now on. We cannot ignore it. It seems to be stronger as we near our destination. I think Man With Many Medicines is getting bolder and wants to defeat us."

Sacred Bird sat, weighed the words of Eagle Crier, and wondered, 'How will Sacred Feather Woman make it back to our people if I don't make it?' She spoke up after a while and turned to Eagle Crier and his wife, "If I don't make it to our people, would you . . ."

Eagle Crier turned and held his hand up to prevent her from finishing what she wanted to ask. Sacred Bird looked at him and Walks With Porcupine Woman, both had pity in their eyes.

He took a deep breath and said, "No, don't even think of not making it, you will make it to our people; we will all make it." He paused and then continued, "Let us all try not to think of this evil that we are up against. Just think of making a safe and happy journey back to our people."

They did not have too much to eat that morning as they set out for the day. The provisions were considerably less than what they had when they set out. As they walked, Sacred Bird took in the surrounding land. As she looked to the north, she saw the storm clouds in the horizon and pointed them out to Eagle Crier and Walks With Porcupine Woman. Both looked at each other and said that it might be nightfall before the storm hit them and by then they would have built a shelter. In the meantime, they should try to go as far as possible.

It was cold. Sacred Bird told her daughter to try not to breathe in the cold air and to cover her face as much as possible. Sacred Bird tried not to breathe in the cold air too much, but it was very difficult to cover her face and carry the load. They travelled at a brisk pace, and she knew both Sacred Feather Woman and Walks With Porcupine Woman must be exhausted as she was. Sacred Bird could barely keep up. They walked in a single file; Eagle Crier was in the lead and Sacred Bird was last.

They had walked down a hill and as she looked ahead, she was relieved to see trees. This place had many hills and trees. The north wind had arrived, and its chilly fingers seemed to prod them along to quicken their pace. Sacred Bird's face felt numb from the cold, and she could not see clearly because of the tears that were threatening to freeze if she did not wipe them.

They walked in silence until they reached the trees. The trees had white bark, which seemed to be invisible against the white snow, and only their branches seemed to reach out to greet them. Eagle Crier led them through the trees, and they silently followed. Their legs seemed to resist the journey by giving out. They would take turns tripping over any object that happened to be in their way.

They reached a little clearing and by then the storm was almost upon them. They could hear the roar of the wind as it approached them at a much faster pace. Eagle Crier had to shout so that they could hear. They strained to hear what he was saying, and Sacred Bird nodded as if she understood what he was saying. Sacred Bird turned to Sacred Feather Woman, who had fallen behind, and motioned for her to go in front of her. The turn towards the north wind almost made her lose her balance. The icy wind on her forehead and cheeks felt like someone had slapped her. She turned quickly and held her head down.

Sacred Bird guided her daughter. They followed Eagle Crier and Walks With Porcupine Woman into the woods. Walking through these woods was difficult enough, but the snow and wind seemed to push Sacred Bird from behind as if to tell her to hurry. Sacred Bird let the wind carry her along, but she had to watch her steps so as not to trip over the many branches that were strewn along the way.

She felt the wind on her legs and knew that the leggings were coming undone. She had to hurry along so that she could tie them. Eagle Crier led them to a clearing. He had started to gather the branches and was leaning them against the tall swaying trees. Sacred Bird was not quite sure why he was laying the branches against the trees.

She put her load by Walks With Porcupine Woman and Sacred Feather Woman and proceeded to help Eagle Crier set up the tepee. She proceeded to do the same, gathering and putting the large branches up against the tall tree.

CHAPTER 11

HARDSHIP AND LOSS

The little tepee was warm and cosy that night. Everyone was content to sit in silence as they ate their small meal. They listened to the fierceness of the storm outside. Sacred Bird wondered if the events of the night before were going to be repeated. She closed her eyes and silently prayed that they would have a peaceful night. They needed a peaceful night to rest and be rejuvenated for the next part of the journey.

Eagle Crier finished his meal and noisily moved around to a more comfortable position to relax for the night. Walks with Porcupine Woman seemed to be enjoying her meal and did not say anything. Sacred Feather Woman had finished her meal and looked like she was ready to doze off. Sacred Bird finished her meal and helped her daughter get comfortable for the night.

As she brushed her daughter's hair away from her eyes, she felt Sacred Feather Woman's forehead. Her daughter was feverish.

Sacred Bird bent down and whispered, "You are going to be all right by morning. I will make sure you are warm during the night, do not be afraid to wake me during the night if I fall asleep." Sacred Feather Woman nodded and closed her eyes.

Sacred Bird was worried about her daughter and decided to stay up. She decided to tell Eagle Crier and his wife that Sacred Feather Woman was feverish. She wanted Eagle Crier and his wife to pray for her daughter before they went to sleep for the night.

She turned to Eagle Crier. "My daughter is feverish, I don't think I will sleep this night," she said as she stroked Sacred Feather Woman's hair to help her daughter to relax and fall asleep.

Eagle Crier and Walks With Porcupine Woman both spoke at the same time, stopped and looked at each other, and started again. Walks With Porcupine Woman stopped and smiled at her husband and pointed to him to talk first.

Eagle Crier smiled and started to talk, saying, "I think that it is better to take turns sleeping tonight. We can each take turns feeding the fire to keep warm throughout the night and making sure that Sacred Feather Woman has a good night's rest. That way we all get a little sleep tonight and no one is deprived of any sleep. We cannot take a chance to have another one of us getting sick."

Walks With Porcupine Woman nodded and agreed with her husband. She turned to Sacred Bird and smiled and said, "I would like to say that maybe we should stay in this place until the storm subsides. I do not think it would be wise for Sacred Feather Woman to travel in this weather. Just to make sure she does not get any worse."

Sacred Bird agreed and told them she would be the first to watch and feed the fire. The others nodded and smiled. Eagle Crier suggested they pray and then they could relax. He reached into his bag and prepared for the prayers. They sat in silence as Eagle Crier moved a little closer to the fire and laid out small amounts of the Sweet Grass as if to ration it out for each day. He proceeded to say his prayers as the sweet aroma of the Sweet Grass filled the little tepee.

Sacred Bird closed her eyes and prayed. She felt a peace come over her as she prayed; she hoped that the peaceful feeling was also felt by Sacred Feather Woman. It had been a long time since she felt the peaceful feeling, it seemed to cover her from her head to the tips of her toes. She wanted that feeling to stay with her throughout the night. She sat there with her eyes closed for the duration of Eagle Crier's prayer, just relaxing and enjoying the moment.

When Eagle Crier finished his prayers, he put the Sweet Grass back into the bag and put the bag away. He looked at the others and got into a comfortable position. He spoke to them and said, "Tomorrow we will decide if we should go on or if we should stay here, it will depend on the storm." Walks With Porcupine Woman and Sacred Bird both nodded and said yes to him.

That night, the three of them took turns keeping watch. Creator heard their prayers. The frightful events did not return that night. Everyone had their rest. Sacred Feather Woman was still feverish, but she was able to sleep. She did, however, tell her mother that she felt cold. Sacred Bird rubbed her daughter's feet to warm them and then piled another robe on her for more warmth.

The next day the wind blew noisily through the trees as the day before. Sacred Bird decided to venture out and look for dried wood. She got ready to go out. She put on her leggings extra tight so the snow would not get on her ankles. Next, she put on her robe over her head and body and held tightly.

As soon as she got out, she felt the fury of the wind; it blew snow into all the little openings of her garment. She knew that this would not be a good day to travel. She ran to a group of trees she had seen the day before. She had noticed that the trees had a few branches bare of bark, and they would make a good fire. She started to collect the dead branches and a few that were sticking out of the snow. She grabbed as many as she could. She could not stand the biting wind on her exposed skin, but she did manage to get enough firewood.

On her way back to the little tepee, she glanced around and did not notice any movement or animals. She felt satisfied that they would be safe here for another day. She got in and made sure the flap was secured to keep out the cold. She fed the dying fire. In no time, the little tepee was warm. Sacred Bird searched the pouches for meat. She found the meat and decided to cook it. Maybe the aroma of the food would wake the others up. The food in the pouch was not much, but it should last maybe another day. She knew that on the days they do not travel, they eat less to conserve the food.

After a short while, Eagle Crier and Walks With Porcupine Woman stirred and got up. Both were in a good mood, which was a good sign. Sacred Bird knew this day would be good for them all. Eagle Crier said he would go out and find out what the day would be like. He left a short time later. He was gone for a long while and when he came back, he told the others that this day was not good for travelling. The storm might stop later in the day; if it stopped, the night would be very cold. It was best they stay another day to be safe.

Walks With Porcupine Woman suggested they each take turns getting firewood to last until the next day. She said, "I am sure tomorrow will be a better day for travelling."

Eagle Crier replied, "You are right, but I would suggest you two take turns getting the firewood and I will look for small game so we will not starve."

Sacred Bird joined in the conversation, "Yes, that is a good idea. Earlier, when I went out, I did not see any animals out there. Maybe they are all like us, staying put to keep warm."

She then turned and felt Sacred Feather Woman's forehead to see if the fever had left. Sacred Feather Woman's forehead was still warm, but not as hot as the night before. Sacred Bird felt relieved to know that the fever might be gone later in the day. She did not have to worry about Sacred Feather Woman's fever getting any worse. She thanked the Creator for the answered prayers.

After they ate, Eagle Crier got ready to go out and hunt. He did not know what he would be looking for but was hopeful to come back with something. He was no stranger to hunting, but it was a challenge this time. He did not have the proper weapons to hunt as he did when he was with the people in the home camp. He looked around and smiled at his wife and left.

Walks With Porcupine Woman smiled at Sacred Bird and said, "I don't have to worry about not having food with Eagle Crier around. He always comes home with food. He is a good man."

Sacred Bird nodded her head and said, "I know he is a good man. You are very fortunate. I have noticed that he is a good provider. He seems to know how to get the game. Maybe you better sharpen your knife. He will be successful and come back with game. I hope he comes back with a deer. Deer are very good. I will go out and get the firewood." Sacred Bird retied her leggings as securely as she could.

Walks With Porcupine Woman agreed and proceeded to sharpen her knife. She took out the knife and laid it on the ground and then searched her pouch for the little rock she used to sharpen her knife.

It was getting late in the day when Eagle Crier returned. He came back with a small rabbit. Walks With Porcupine Woman was delighted with the small game. She seemed to enjoy cooking for her husband. Sacred Bird fed the fire and was content to sit and wait for the meal. The little tepee was cosy and warm; Sacred Bird felt comfortable and was able to relax.

Sacred Feather Woman was still lying down. She seemed content not to move a muscle. Sacred Bird did not urge her to get up. It seemed pointless to, as space in the tepee was so tiny; there was no room to move around too much.

The aroma of Walks With Porcupine Woman's cooking filled the little tepee. For the first time, Sacred Bird looked forward to the meal. The idea of eating rabbit did not turn her stomach. She was getting used to eating strange meat. Walks With Porcupine Woman had a special way of making the meals she prepared appetizing by using the special dried leaves she carried with her.

After the meal, they all sat and talked about the next part of the journey and, with excitement, their destination. Eagle Crier said he was looking forward to seeing his family after four winters. He was excited to introduce his wife to his parents and other members of the family for the first time since he left. Walks With Porcupine Woman, on the other hand, was very nervous about meeting Eagle Crier's family. She said she was not sure if they would approve of her.

At that, Sacred Bird asked Eagle Crier how he came to be at the northern camp. Eagle Crier smiled and said, "I will tell you all about it when we get to our destination. It is a little complicated."

This got Sacred Bird very curious. She could not wait to get to their destination. She too had a story to tell, but then, she had already told her story to Eagle Crier and Walks With Porcupine Woman. Sacred Bird sat back and looked at Eagle Crier, "Don't forget to tell me your story. If you do forget, I will remind you."

Eagle Crier smiled and said, "I know I will not forget; you will keep reminding me." With that, Walks With Porcupine Woman portioned the meal and fed everyone.

They ate their fill and then rested. The tepee was warm. Sacred Bird and Eagle Crier each took turns to get wood to feed the fire and keep everyone warm. It was getting dark and there was a slight breeze from the north. Eagle Crier told them that if the weather was good, they would travel the next day. He said he hoped the snow was not too deep so they could travel a long distance.

Sacred Bird woke up the next morning before the sun rose. She ventured out to find out how the day was shaping out to be. Although she was not an expert in weather, she guessed it would be a good day to travel. The wind had stopped blowing and the sky was grey with a few clouds. The snow was not too deep.

She went back into the tepee to find everyone still sleeping; she added more wood to the fire to warm the tepee. She decided she would let Walks With Porcupine Woman prepare the meal this morning. She sat and thought about the family she was going home to. What would their reaction be? She knew it would be very emotional. She wondered how Sacred Feather Woman would react and if she would remember everyone. Sacred Bird's thoughts were interrupted by Sacred Feather Woman's coughing.

She turned to Sacred Feather Woman and helped her sit up. Then she searched for the water container. After a few sips, Sacred Feather Woman stopped coughing. Sacred Bird felt Sacred Feather Woman's forehead, she was feverish.

'This is not good,' Sacred Bird thought to herself; 'Sacred Feather Woman may not be fit to travel.'

Sacred Feather Woman's fever would come and go. Each time the fever returned, her cough would be worse than before. This made it harder for Sacred Bird to decide whether they should travel. If they stayed, the weather might be worse, but if they travelled, Sacred Feather Woman's health might get worse. Sacred Bird decided to let Eagle Crier know. Maybe he would have an idea to keep Sacred Feather Woman warm as they travelled.

After discussing this with Eagle Crier and his wife, both suggested they could still travel. They could make a travois for Sacred Feather Woman to ride in and stay warm. This was a good idea. Eagle Crier said he would find two poles and make the travois for their belongings and Sacred Feather Woman.

It did not take long for Eagle Crier to find two poles. Walks With Porcupine Woman was adept at making the travois comfortable and secure for a person and a load. Sacred Feather Woman was delighted to ride. Eagle Crier said he would pull it as he didn't think Walks With Porcupine Woman or Sacred Bird would be able to pull it. Both women suggested they could help in some way to make it easier for Eagle Crier by walking on either side to lift the back end of the two poles with a rope if they needed to. This was a good idea, and they were able to travel quite a distance that day.

It was almost dark by the time they found a good spot to camp for the night. The place they found was at the bottom of a little hill, which had a few trees and bushes. Eagle Crier proceeded to make the shelter with the help of both women. Sacred Bird found a good place for Sacred Feather Woman to sit with the robe around her to keep her warm.

After the shelter was made, they started a fire in the middle of the shelter for warmth, and it was cosy. Walks With Porcupine Woman made the meal for everyone. Sacred Bird gathered the wood for the fire after she made Sacred Feather Woman comfortable and warm. Eagle Crier was able to rest.

They ate the delicious meal that Walks With Porcupine Woman had prepared and got comfortably settled in for the night. Sacred Bird was worried about her little daughter. Sacred Feather Woman was running a fever and her breathing was laboured. Sacred Bird informed Eagle Crier and Walks With Porcupine Woman that she would stay up throughout the night to keep an eye on her daughter. Both Eagle Crier and his wife were concerned and offered to stay up part of the night with her. Sacred Bird was thankful for their offers and accepted. She did not want anything to happen to her daughter, their help would ease her anxiety.

Eagle Crier and his wife took turns getting the firewood and feeding the fire throughout the night, while Sacred Bird watched over her daughter. She hoped that Sacred Feather Woman's fever would break by morning. She had to soothe and rock her daughter and try to make her as comfortable as possible. Sacred Feather Woman seemed to be in pain. The only thing that Sacred Bird could do was pray.

Eagle Crier and his wife dozed off for a bit and Sacred Bird did not disturb them. She knew it was almost morning. Her hope was that with daybreak, Sacred Feather Woman's fever would break and feel much better. That was what she was praying for. But by morning Sacred Feather Woman was still the same; Sacred Bird started to panic. She finally woke Eagle Crier and his wife.

They woke up and felt Sacred Feather Woman's forehead. They suggested maybe they should not travel that day. They suggested that Sacred Bird give her daughter some cool water to try and cool her body. Sacred Feather Woman's fever was way too high. That day, they all tried different methods to get the fever down, but none worked. They prayed, and they cooled her body down by taking the covers off, all to no avail.

There was a short time that Sacred Feather Woman seemed to come out of it. She sat up and asked for water. They happily obliged and then she said she was hungry. They finely chopped the meat they had prepared and fed her. Everyone was elated that Sacred Feather Woman was getting better. Sacred Bird was happy, and she could not contain her happiness; she hugged and kissed her daughter and told her how much she loved her.

They went about doing their chores throughout the day. Sacred Bird was beside her daughter all that day. Sacred Feather Woman's fever seemed to be going away and then would return. This upset Sacred Bird, she did not know what to make of it. Her hopes would be dashed every time her daughter's fever returned and then she would panic. The ups and downs of her emotions took their toll on Sacred Bird and made her body weak.

It was the third day that Sacred Feather Woman went into a deep sleep. Sacred Bird prayed, cried, and felt so lost. She noticed that Sacred Feather Woman's breathing was laboured, and this alarmed Sacred Bird. She knew what was going to happen if her daughter did not come out, but she tried to reassure herself.

'Sacred Feather Woman will get better,' she told herself. But it was not to be.

Late that night, Sacred Feather Woman took her last breath. Sacred Bird was so devastated that she could not remember that night or the next day. Eagle Crier and Walks With Porcupine Woman took care of Sacred Bird as best they could. They also took care to place Sacred Feather Woman's remains in a tree far from the little tepee. They had done a little ceremony that Sacred Bird was present for but was not conscious of.

The next two days, Sacred Bird was still in mourning, but she had started to remember the events of her daughter's death. She did not, however, remember that this was the fourth day since the death. Eagle Crier and his wife did everything they could to take care of Sacred Bird, and their efforts were paying off. Sacred Bird was coming out of the traumatic experience. She was aware of what had happened and what needed to happen.

Sacred Bird went to where Sacred Feather Woman's body was and mourned for most of the day. Eagle Crier and Walks With Porcupine Woman allowed her to go through this, making sure that Sacred Bird was safe. While Sacred Bird was at Sacred Feather Woman's resting site, Eagle Crier and his wife prepared for the journey ahead. They had to leave and could not spend another day at this place.

It took a lot of coaxing and pleading to get Sacred Bird to leave her daughter. Eagle Crier and his wife understood what Sacred Bird was going through and they were patient with her. They managed to get Sacred Bird to start walking away from Sacred Feather Woman. Sacred Bird, on the other hand, could not understand and refused to accept the death of her daughter.

Eagle Crier spoke a few words to Sacred Feather Woman. He asked her to assist them on the journey since she had crossed over and was no longer hindered by the weather or her sickness. This brought Sacred Bird back to the present and she cried even more. Walks With Porcupine Woman gently took Sacred Bird by the elbow and steered her along.

Both Eagle Crier and Walks With Porcupine Woman walked in silence. Sacred Bird also walked in silence except to make sobbing noises. Sacred Bird could not stop mourning for her daughter. They had spent every day together since they had left the home camp. Sacred Bird had depended on her daughter for comfort, companionship, and encouragement. Sacred Feather Woman had been there to provide emotional support throughout the journey.

CHAPTER 12

HARSH JOURNEY AND LOSS

Sacred Bird woke that first morning in the new camp site and felt an overwhelming sense of emptiness. She had been silent except to clear her throat after weeping in silence. She did not know if she would ever stop crying. Crying seemed to be a part of her daily ritual. Sometimes the tears would come without warning. The hardest part of her day was when they were making the shelter for the night. She was used to making Sacred Feather Woman comfortable and now she had no one.

The weather had been agreeable the past five days, which made it easier for Eagle Crier and his wife to move the shelter without Sacred Bird's help. They had used the travois to transport their belongings. Sacred Bird had no recollection of how she made it to this place. Sacred Bird did not particularly want to know. She did, however, appreciate Eagle Crier and his wife for taking care of her.

Sacred Bird wiped her tears and decided to go out and check the weather and the surroundings. She tried to convince herself that she must make every effort to be part of the team and help as best she can. She emerged from the small tepee to find the sky cloudy. The cold air made her shiver. She held her robe tightly and walked over to some trees that stood not too far from the shelter.

She proceeded to take some dried branches and place them by the shelter. She took a walk toward a small hill on the other side of the trees. It took a little time to climb the hill. She reached the top, and to her surprise she could see over the snow blowing across the land to distant hills. She did not recognize the land. This land seemed so desolate, so lonely. Seeing the desolate land had an adverse effect on her and she decided to head back to the shelter. She looked for any animal tracks, but of course there would not be any because the wind would cover them with snow.

She got back to the shelter and found that Eagle Crier and his wife were awake. Eagle Crier and Walks With Porcupine Woman greeted her with smiles and told her they were glad she was up and about. Walks With Porcupine Woman happily started to make a meal, while Eagle Crier got ready to head out in search of more firewood. Sacred Bird added the wood she got to the fire. She sat down and looked at Walks With Porcupine Woman and told her how much she appreciated their care while she was mourning her daughter. Walks With Porcupine Woman did not wait for her to finish; in a soothing voice, she told Sacred Bird that she understood what she went through. They felt they had to take care of Sacred Bird because she is family.

With that, Sacred Bird could not help it, the tears came again. Walks With Porcupine Woman patted her shoulder and did not try to stop her. In a soothing voice, Walks With Porcupine Woman encouraged her to let the tears out. Walks With Porcupine Woman tended to her cooking. By then, Eagle Crier returned with an armload of firewood. Sacred Bird had gotten rid of the tears and had composed herself.

Eagle Crier sat across from Sacred Bird and, with a smile, asked if they were ready to move out as soon as the meal was over. He said the weather should be ok to travel. It would not storm until later in the day. In fact, it might be nightfall before a storm came. They could travel a long distance since the snow was not deep and the wind was not that strong. Walks With Porcupine Woman agreed as she served the meal, adding that they would have to get more food.

They ate their meal in silence and then got ready to go on their journey. Each knew what had to be done. In no time, the little shelter was down and packed. There had not been any laughter for a long time. and it showed in their movement. Their steps were heavier and strenuous. Sacred Bird noticed and she did not try to lighten the mood. Each step she took was a struggle; she knew it was not because of the snow, which had hardened under the force of the wind.

The journey was slow, walking against the wind and blowing snow. Sacred Bird had to cover her mouth as best she could. She did not know how far they had travelled but she was thankful when Eagle Crier stopped and said they should look for a good place to put up the shelter for the night. As he looked up at the sky, he went on to say that the weather might turn for the worse later. The place they selected to camp was littered with bushes and a few trees.

Walks With Porcupine Woman agreed with her husband and suggested that Eagle Crier look for small game as soon as they finished putting up the shelter. They worked in silence, except when Eagle Crier gave instructions as they set up the shelter. Sacred Bird proceeded to look for firewood. All she could find were the slender branches of the bushes and a few large branches from the trees.

Walks With Porcupine Woman was left alone in the shelter to prepare the few items to make the beds. They had very few robes and would need a fire all night to keep warm. She, too, was coming down with a cold. She did not tell the others how she felt. She busied herself by taking care of the meal.

Sacred Bird returned with the firewood and sat and waited for the fire to warm the little shelter. It was quite a while before Eagle Crier returned with a rabbit. It seemed that was the only game available in this part of the land. Sacred Bird longed for a better meal. That longing brought loneliness for the home she had been taken from. She tried to remember a meal with her family at the home camp. Eagle Crier and Walks With Porcupine Woman, on the other hand, were conversing happily as they prepared the rabbit.

Walks With Porcupine Woman was very efficient at cutting up the meat to portions for easy storage. Both seemed so happy. Sacred Bird longed to be happy again. She tried to join the conversation but each time she tried, she could not find the words to say, so she kept quiet.

Both Eagle Crier and his wife did not seem to mind. They continued talking about how Eagle Crier got the rabbit. He was telling his wife that he was getting good at throwing the walking stick his wife used to knock out the rabbit. Then he added maybe it was the soft and hard snow that made it difficult for the rabbit to run fast.

That night the wind howled, and they knew the storm had arrived. Sacred Bird was content to listen to the storm outside. There was enough firewood to keep warm during the night, she would venture out in the morning to get more. Eagle Crier took out his Sweet Grass, which was almost gone, and smudged and prayed. The prayers seemed to lighten the atmosphere. Sacred Bird joined in on the conversation that Eagle Crier and his wife were having. She even laughed at the funny stories they were telling.

It was not morning yet when Eagle Crier woke her. He whispered that the strange noises were back. Sacred Bird's heart sank as she sat up and listened to the now familiar noises. She was not sure who the target would be. She whispered to Eagle Crier that they should use the Sweet Grass. Eagle Crier got the Sweet Grass and got ready to pray, while Walks With Porcupine Woman sat comfortably next to him. They sat and prayed. This time Sacred Bird was willing to sacrifice herself, but she did not tell this to Eagle Crier.

She had accepted defeat. She could not and would not let either Eagle Crier or his wife be taken away. The loss of two children had been a costly blow to them. For some reason, Eagle Crier looked at Sacred Bird and encouraged her to pray. He told her not to give up. Sacred Bird just nodded.

Eagle Crier did not stop encouraging her. He told Sacred Bird, "The expression on your face tells me that you have given up! You cannot give up! You have to fight; you have other children at the home camp who want you to live."

Sacred Bird prayed and did not tell Eagle Crier that she had given up. It seemed like her whole world was collapsing, and she did not have the energy to fight. She closed her eyes and attempted to pray, but her attempts were interrupted by the images of her daughter. After struggling with the images, she finally let out a cry to the Creator. She struggled with the images.

Eagle Crier and Walks With Porcupine Woman tried to comfort her, but the noises were getting closer, and this time they took on a more ominous sound. Sacred Bird did not know at that time, but Eagle Crier and Walks With Porcupine Woman had heard her words. The words would be unsettling to Eagle Crier and his wife. They would have to wait for a more favourable time when the threats were over to discuss Sacred Bird's words.

Sacred Bird knew all too well what happens when the 'noises' arrive. She was the target and she dreaded having to go through the pain. She cried out to the Creator to take her out of this situation. She did not know how else she could stand the pain that came when these creatures attacked. She also knew that she would be out for a while.

Eagle Crier and his wife continued to pray. They were accustomed to these attacks, and they knew they would have to be strong for Sacred Bird. They did not know how severe the attack would be, but they would be ready. The noises came in a rush and Sacred Bird braced herself. She did not remember the rest of that night.

She woke up that morning as if someone touched her shoulder to wake her up. She opened her eyes and looked around to see if anyone had touched her shoulder, but she was the only one awake. The light in the little shelter was dim; the fire had almost gone out, just the red embers were keeping the shelter warm, and it was getting cold. She pulled the robe closer around her to warm herself. She had no energy to get up. She looked over to Eagle Crier and his wife; they were both still sleeping.

She tried to remember yesterday. As she was thinking about the events of the evening, she heard Eagle Crier stir. She did not want to let him know that she was awake. Eagle Crier got up and added wood to the fire. In no time the little shelter lit up brightly with the fire. She heard Walks With Porcupine Woman call her husband. Eagle Crier answered, and they both talked in low voices; Sacred Bird could not make out what they were saying.

In a short while, Eagle Crier went outside and Walks With Porcupine Woman followed her husband. They were gone for a while; Sacred Bird debated whether she should get up and finally decided to start her day. For some reason she did not want to know what happened during the night. She knew she had to deal with the events that keep happening, but the hardest part of the events was that she could not remember. She wished she had something she could use to combat the attacks. She knew this was not a good way to deal with them, almost as if she was taking the cowardly way out.

The little shelter was nice and warm. Sacred Bird felt comfortable to sit and ponder what she had to do. She had no idea what she should do. She had always relied on the Elders to help her out with things like this. She wished she knew what to do and how to deal with this feeling of uncertainty.

Eagle Crier and his wife came back and added more wood to the fire. They were delighted to see Sacred Bird sitting up. Eagle Crier sat down and asked Sacred Bird how she was feeling. Walks With Porcupine Woman smiled and said she was glad to see Sacred Bird up. Walks With Porcupine Woman told Sacred Bird that they had been worried, but she knew Sacred Bird would come out of the sleep. This time it took Sacred Bird three days to come out of it.

Walks With Porcupine Woman described how she and Eagle Crier would get up in the middle of the night to check on her. They knew she would wake up sooner or later because her breathing was normal. Walks With Porcupine Woman said, "I just don't understand why this man is so upset you left. He had many women."

Eagle Crier did not hesitate and suggested an answer, "Maybe this man has never lost to anyone, not even a woman. He is used to having his way."

Sacred Bird did not have answers. She, too, had wondered. This was something that Sacred Bird must think about to find a way not to be defeated. She vowed to herself that from now on she would do everything in her power not to let Man With Many Medicines get his way. Sacred Bird said, "I must not let my guard down, I must be vigilant," and with that she thanked Eagle Crier and his wife for taking care of her.

She apologized to them for giving up. She told Eagle Crier, "I am very sorry, I should not have given up, and I am sorry for putting you and your wife in danger. I didn't know that Man With Many Medicines would be so determined to go after me."

Eagle Crier sat for a while before offering his opinion. "I think that Man With Many Medicines is trying to break you into returning to him. He will not rest until he wins. You must make up your mind and fight back. Think back and see if you have had any visions or dreams. You must have had a dream since you came to be with Man With Many Medicines. Maybe you did not think it was of any significance, but once you remember, maybe you can take some direction from it."

For the next few days, Sacred Bird thought about what Eagle Crier had talked about. For the first time in the past few days, Sacred Bird cried and could not stop the tears. Her tears came because she thought about Sacred Feather Woman. She had told her daughter about the dreams she had, and Sacred Feather Woman had a good memory. If she were here, she would be able to tell her about some of the dreams that Sacred Bird told her about. But since Sacred Feather Woman was not there anymore, Sacred Bird would have to remember the details herself.

Thinking about Sacred Feather Woman brought tears, which Sacred Bird had a hard time stopping. It seemed that the more she wanted them to stop, the more they came. Eagle Crier and Walks With Porcupine Woman sat in silence, letting Sacred Bird cry. They knew that the tears had to be let out.

After she cried, Sacred Bird sat and thought about the happy times she had with Sacred Feather Woman. Her daughter was gentle and wise for her young age. Her companionship was going to be missed. Sacred Bird could talk to her about anything and she would understand. Sacred Feather Woman had often offered her opinions about the topics that were discussed. She had a way with words; although only a few, she always made sense.

Eagle Crier broke the silence and suggested they break camp and continue the journey. It was a good day to travel. The wind was not strong, and it would be wise to travel that day and maybe travel as far as possible.

Both women began to pack the meagre belongings and start the journey. They used the travois; it was a good way to carry the belongings. They started out on the journey, heading in a westerly direction. Sacred Bird was able to see the horizon and could make out the mountains, but she could not recognize them. She walked behind the travois that Eagle Crier and his wife were pulling.

As she walked, she thought about Sacred Feather Woman. Oh, how she missed her daughter. She could just picture her sitting on the travois, smiling and in good spirits. She wondered how her family at the home camp would receive the news of Sacred Feather Woman's death, especially the old folks. They were the ones who had spent many days with her, and they were the ones who were responsible for Sacred Feather Woman's gentleness. They taught her to be gentle, kind, and caring. Sacred Bird knew they would be devastated.

As for her husband, he would also be devastated. He had taken pride in having a beautiful daughter that he could dote on. Sacred Bird remembered the day Sacred Feather Woman was born. Her husband had taken her in is his arms and immediately started talking to her, making plans for her. He even suggested that she would be the envy of all the little girls in the clan. Sacred Bird did not realize it, but thinking about that day brought a smile. Those were the good memories that she would cherish for the rest of her life.

Eagle Crier and his wife noticed Sacred Bird's smile, but they did not ask why she was smiling. That is how Eagle Crier and his wife were. They had great respect for others, and they knew that Sacred Bird would share her thoughts when she was ready. They did, however, smile with her. They knew that whatever the thought was, it was a good one.

CHAPTER 13

LONELY JOURNEY

*E*agle Crier and his wife stopped three times to rest. Sacred Bird knew they were getting tired, but there was a look of determination on Eagle Crier's face. He had walked along a small ridge for a while. He was clearly looking for a suitable camp site. Both women did not offer a suggestion; they just followed along as if in a daze. They were tired from the journey. They had not suggested they stop, which was unusual.

Eagle Crier broke the silence. He suggested they help gather all the long sticks they could find for the shelter. Without a word, Walks With Porcupine Woman and Sacred Bird proceeded to walk to a group of bushes. Meanwhile, Eagle Crier had walked away to look for a suitable place to put up the shelter.

Both women gathered as many sticks as they could find and piled them up in one place for Eagle Crier to choose the ones he could use. He called them and asked them if they could carry them, as he had found a suitable place among the bushes. He returned to retrieve the travois. The site he chose was in between thick bushes that would help keep the wind out. Walks with Porcupine Woman picked up the sticks she gathered and slowly walked over to the site that Eagle Crier had chosen. Sacred Bird also picked up her load and proceeded to the chosen site.

Eagle Crier looked at both women with a puzzled look but did not say anything. He knew they were tired. He also knew that he had not offered to give them rest sooner, so he concluded that he would apologize to them when they settled in. He busied himself with making the shelter. It took him a long time to finish the shelter. Most of the sticks the women brought were too short or too flimsy, he had to tie them together to make them a little stronger.

It was getting dark when Eagle Crier finally finished the shelter, and by that time he was exhausted. Walks With Porcupine Woman asked Sacred Bird if she could make the meal, she said she was completely without energy. Sacred Bird, although very tired, happily obliged and made the meal. Not too many words were said that night. They were all exhausted and turned in for the night.

The next morning, Sacred Bird woke to a very cold shelter. She added wood to the embers. It took a bit of coaxing to get the fire going. After she was sure the fire would not die down, she got ready to go out.

The cold air took her breath away as she emerged from the shelter. There was a slight breeze, and she wrapped her robe closer to keep out the cold. She surveyed her surroundings and turned to the right to go around the shelter so that she could look past the bushes. She saw movement in the distant hill. She took a few more steps to take a better look at the movement. The animal looked like a deer. Her heart raced; she had not seen a deer for quite a while. In fact, this was the first deer she had seen in so many days, she had forgotten when she last saw one. She stood for a while gazing at the deer, wondering if she would ever taste deer again. She took a few more steps and when she looked again, the deer was gone.

After wandering around the bushes, she decided she would collect a few dried branches and return to the shelter. Spending time alone outside the shelter made her think of Sacred Feather Woman, and when she thought of her, tears would well up in her eyes. Not wanting to cry, she quickly wiped the tears away and went back to the shelter. Sacred Bird knew that thinking of Sacred Feather Woman would bring a lot of tears and she did not want to start crying. Sacred Feather Woman was very special, missing her brought a lot of pain.

Sacred Bird returned to the shelter to find Eagle Crier and his wife still asleep. Sacred Bird did not want to make any unnecessary noise to wake them, so she quietly added wood to the fire. The shelter was still a bit cool, and she wanted to warm up after being out in the cold. She sat in silence and pondered what might have been if Sacred Feather Woman had not passed away. She would be preparing a meal for her, or she would be covering her up to keep her warm on this cool morning. Sacred Bird shook her head and decided she would try to stay focussed on the next part of the journey. She desperately needed to make it to the home camp.

A short while later, Eagle Crier stirred and sat up. He was surprised that Sacred Bird was already up. Sacred Bird smiled at him and said, "You two must have been really tired to sleep so long. I have been up for a while. It is a good thing I woke up because it was really cold in here."

Eagle Crier replied, "Yes, I was tired, but Walks With Porcupine Woman was up for most of the night. She had a high fever, and I could not help her. I think she was up for a long time. I am not sure if we will go on. We will see if she is fit to travel, otherwise we will have to stay here until she is well enough to travel."

Sacred Bird knew all too well that they would be spending a few days there if Walks With Porcupine Woman didn't get well. A fever does not go away in a day unless it is treated. She told Eagle Crier that she would prepare the meal. With that, Sacred Bird took the bags containing the meat. To her disappointment, there was very little food left. She told Eagle Crier that they only had one meal left.

Eagle Crier said he would go out and look for food as soon as Walks With Porcupine Woman woke up. He wanted to make sure that Walks With Porcupine Woman knew where he was going and also to make sure his wife was not too sick. Eagle Crier and Sacred Bird sat in silence until Walks With Porcupine Woman woke up.

Eagle Crier tended to his wife, making sure that Walks With Porcupine Woman was up for a little walk outside. Her fever was not completely gone, she shivered and agreed to go out. Eagle Crier asked Sacred Bird to add a little more wood to the fire to heat the shelter more. Sacred Bird did what was requested of her and kept the fire going until the shelter was nice and warm for Walks With Porcupine Woman. She had prepared the meal and waited for them to return.

After a short while, Eagle Crier and his wife returned. Walks With Porcupine Woman was shivering and Eagle Crier piled the robes on top of her to warm her. Sacred Bird knew then that Walks With Porcupine Woman would not be fit to travel. She would get worse if they tried to travel in the cold. Sacred Bird decided she would gather more wood for the fire later.

She told Eagle Crier about the deer she saw earlier when she went out. Eagle Crier said he did not know if he could get a deer without any weapons. With that, Sacred Bird was willing to cook whatever Eagle Crier could get; however, she was not looking forward to a rabbit meal for the next few days. She did not tell Eagle Crier how she felt about the rabbit.

Eagle Crier went out and came back with a rabbit. Sacred Bird skinned and prepared the rabbit. This time there were no happy voices in the shelter when the rabbit was being prepared. Sacred Bird worked in silence while Eagle Crier tended to his wife, making her as comfortable as possible. Walks With Porcupine Woman did not talk much, she would only answer Eagle Crier when he asked her a question.

Two nights later, the weather turned ugly outside. The winds picked up, howling through the bushes, and the snow fell but did not stay on the ground. The wind would pick it up and toss it away. The snow that stayed on the ground was held back by the bushes. By morning there was a huge snowdrift on either side of the entrance to the little shelter.

Walks With Porcupine Woman was not getting any better. She had gotten worse. She could barely talk, and she could barely move without a loud groan. Eagle Crier was getting tired, but he would not leave his wife's side. Sacred Bird was the only one out and about, getting little twigs for the fire and keeping the shelter warm. Firewood was getting scarce and Sacred Bird had to go far from the shelter to find wood that would burn. Sacred Bird was getting exhausted. It was hard to walk in the snow drifts to get the wood.

Sacred Bird knew they would all suffer if she did not keep the shelter warm. The weather was very unforgiving. Most of the time they were all silent, except when Walks With Porcupine Woman needed a drink of water. Eagle Crier would immediately tend to her needs and make her comfortable. Sacred Bird could tell that Eagle Crier was getting worn out, he moved slower than usual. He would fall asleep while holding his wife's hand.

Sacred Bird was getting worried for Walks With Porcupine Woman. She should have started to feel better by now; it had been three days since she was unable to get up. The weather was another factor to Sacred Bird's worries. The wind had been blowing and the snow had been coming down since the day after they arrived. Sacred Bird knew something was amiss, but she could not remember what was missing. She sat and pondered for a while, her thoughts getting interrupted by Walks With Porcupine Woman's groans.

She must have fallen asleep because the next thing she knew, Eagle Crier was sobbing. He had Walks With Porcupine Woman in his arms while talking to her. His words were inaudible, but he was clearly pleading for his wife to come back.

Sacred Bird sat up. A feeling of panic came over her. It seemed as if her body could not move in a normal way but in slow motion. She felt a tingling on her back and a feeling of dread.

'This can't be! This is not happening!' she thought to herself. She was finally able to reach across to Eagle Crier to comfort him. As soon as she touched his arm, she could not control her tears. She broke down and wailed with Eagle Crier.

They sat for a long while, mourning Walks With Porcupine Woman. They had lost track of time before they realized that they had to move on. First, they had to take care of Walks With Porcupine Woman's body. They wrapped her in the robe and tied it as best they could. They both went out of the shelter to look for a suitable place for her. To their dismay, they could not find one. Sacred Bird spoke first, telling Eagle Crier that they would have to leave her in the shelter. This was a stunning suggestion to Eagle Crier, who very much loved his wife. He could not bear the thought of leaving Walks With Porcupine Woman in the shelter. He was silent for a long time. Sacred Bird waited for him to answer. She could not think of any other way to honour the body; there were no trees, just shrubs and bushes, which were not suitable.

After a while, Eagle Crier looked at Sacred Bird and agreed that maybe that was the only way. He walked toward the shelter and did not ask Sacred Bird to accompany him. Sacred Bird knew that this was something Eagle Crier would have to do himself. She stood and waited for him.

The day was almost gone when Eagle Crier came back. He had a robe on and carried one for Sacred Bird. He handed the one robe and two pouches to Sacred Bird and said that they would leave everything else with Walks With Porcupine Woman. He told Sacred Bird that he had secured Walks With Porcupine Woman in the robe they had used as a bed, and he had also secured the shelter.

Sacred Bird did not ask any questions as they walked in silence. They walked the rest of the day, stopping only for a short time. Sacred Bird did not dare ask to stop to rest longer; she was also content to walk as far as possible. Her fingers were beginning to feel numb from the cold and her grip was getting weaker, making it harder to hold onto the robe. Still, she was determined to keep up with Eagle Crier.

Sacred Bird endured the long trek in the dark, and for some reason she did not find the words to comfort Eagle Crier. The evening was getting darker, and it was getting harder to see when Eagle Crier finally suggested they find some shelter. They both looked for a shelter. Eagle Crier found one underneath a bush. This must have been a 'home' for some animal, because the little clearing in the middle of the bushes was well-worn, it almost looked like a big nest.

Eagle Crier proceeded to build a little shelter, using the sticks to weave walls. The wind found the little spaces to blow the snow through. Some of the snow got caught in the spaces. On the other side, he built a fire. That was a very cold night, but Sacred Bird did not complain. She somehow blamed herself. She blamed herself for the deaths and the journey plagued with bad events. What could she have done differently?

That night they both sat next to the fire with their backs to the makeshift shelter of sticks and twigs while the wind howled at their backs. The only protection from the cold was the robes they wrapped around themselves. Sleep would come and go throughout the night. Sacred Bird was determined not to show how uncomfortable she was. She sat with her eyes closed, hoping to get some sleep and rest. She tried not to think of the cold. Sometimes during the night the fire would slowly die out because of the snow falling on it, but Eagle Crier would add a few sticks to keep it going.

Sacred Bird finally fell asleep before morning, and she felt as if she had just closed her eyes when the light of day came. It was still snowing and blowing. She was cold, when she moved she would feel the bite of the cold wind on her feet and legs. She thought of all that had happened. She still could not believe that her daughter was gone. She thought about the baby and Walks With Porcupine Woman. She felt sad and wished they were still with them. She shook her head; she did not want to start the day with tears.

Eagle Crier broke the silence and suggested they head out. This time there was no food, and he did not mention it. Sacred Bird was more than eager to start; maybe the walking would help her to think of things other than the regrets. She got up and stretched, pulling the robe closer to help keep out the cold.

Eagle Crier kicked snow on the fire and they headed out. The journey was in silence. Sacred Bird thought a lot of the events that had happened along the journey. She thought about the 'what ifs.' She was still lost in her thoughts when Eagle Crier went down. He lost his footing and fell and could not get up. He had injured his right ankle.

Sacred Bird rushed to help him stand but he was in so much pain. He told Sacred Bird to leave him there for a while. Sacred Bird sat down beside him.

Eagle Crier held his ankle and told Sacred Bird, "I think my ankle is fractured or severely sprained. I don't think I can walk."

Sacred Bird looked back at the little place they had just left and said, "I think we are too far from the little shelter we left, so we should go a little farther and find a suitable place to rest."

Eagle Crier replied, "Yes, just as soon as I can walk. I do not think I can stand on my ankle. I will need help. Do you think you can help me walk? And in the meantime, I will need to look for a stick to hold onto and put my weight on as I walk."

Sacred Bird replied. "I think I can help. And I do not know where we can find a stick unless we come upon a group of trees. I just hope there are trees up ahead."

Sacred Bird and Eagle Crier travelled quite a distance before they came upon some trees in a little valley. The hill was not too steep. The trees were in the bottom of the little valley. To get to them they had to go down a little hill with small bushes, which made the trek down very cumbersome. There were a few times that Eagle Crier almost lost his balance, and at the same time he almost pulled Sacred Bird down with him. Sacred Bird was getting tired, her legs were losing their strength.

After a long time they finally reached the bottom of the hill, but the trees were still far from them. The snow was still blowing in the wind, and both were getting exhausted. Eagle Crier suggested they rest, but Sacred Bird told him that if they did, she might not be able to get up again. She said they should keep going until they reached the trees. Sacred Bird was exhausted; she did not think she could endure the weight of Eagle Crier on her arm and shoulder.

They finally reached the trees. Sacred Bird made sure Eagle Crier was comfortable before she went to search for a stick to help him walk. She looked and even kicked some snow away from the sticks that were protruding from the ground to see if they were suitable for walking and holding Eagle Crier's weight. She was determined to find one, and after looking in several places she found a stick that would hold Eagle Crier's weight.

Eagle Crier tried the stick and it was suitable. Sacred Bird told him she would collect some more to build a shelter. By the time they built the shelter, it was dark. They had not eaten for three days, and Sacred Bird had no idea how they would survive without Eagle Crier's skills at getting small game. Sacred Bird decided she would try and look for something, even rabbit if she could get one.

She left Eagle Crier to tend to the fire and went to look for a rabbit. She walked so far that when she looked back, she could not see the fire, so she decided she would head back before she got lost. Just as she was walking around some tall trees, some bark fell beside her. She looked up and saw an animal perched on a branch. It looked like a porcupine. She decided to try and get it off the tree. She looked for a straight stick that she could throw like a spear.

She found one and threw it up at the porcupine. After several attempts, she managed to hit it a few times, but the porcupine would not fall. She started to talk to herself. Each time she threw the stick, she would yell at the porcupine to let go of the tree branch. She surprised herself when the porcupine fell. Without wasting another breath, she hit it on the head. The porcupine lay motionless on the ground. Sacred Bird stood looking at it. She hit it once more, just to make sure it was dead and would not retaliate by throwing its quills.

This time she was sure it was dead, so she picked it up very carefully and headed back to the little shelter. Eagle Crier had the fire going. Sacred Bird told Eagle Crier not to add too much of the firewood, to save some to cook the meat. Eagle Crier looked at Sacred Bird and then at the porcupine. His face lit up. He could not wait to skin it and cook it.

Sacred Bird had tasted porcupine before and could not wait to eat it. They sat and prepared the porcupine. Both were silent. Sacred Bird remembered the time when they all sat and laughed as they prepared a porcupine a long time ago. Sacred Bird's thoughts turned to that day, that was a happy time. Sacred Bird's thoughts turned to the happy memories, how could she forget those times and the tragedies that had happened? She could see her daughter's smiling face and she could see Walks With Porcupine Woman with her baby.

Sacred Bird could also hear their laughter. Eagle Crier broke the silence and told Sacred Bird to add more wood to the fire to cook the meat.

Sacred Bird added the wood and again they sat in silence, only the sizzle of the meat roasting on the stick broke the silence. Not too many words were exchanged between the two. Both were engrossed in their thoughts.

Sacred Bird began asking questions in her mind: 'Why did all this happen? Why me? For what reason should I go on? What is the reason Man With Many Medicines is doing these things to us? Why hasn't he caught up with us? Is this his way of torturing me?'

Eagle Crier finished his meal and broke the silence by asking Sacred Bird to pack the rest for later. Sacred Bird only made mumbling sounds to answer Eagle Crier. She knew what he had requested. She took the meat and placed it in her bag. This was one of the bags she had used store all the food when she and Sacred Feather Woman first started out from the northern camp. She wondered how long it had been since they left that camp. She had lost all track of time since that day; she had been eager and happy to leave. She had thought it would not take this long to get back to the home camp. She had thought this journey would be an inconvenience, especially for her daughter, and she would have done anything to make the journey easy for her daughter.

CHAPTER 14

ALMOST HOME

The next day, they started early. Their journey would take longer. Eagle Crier was in pain, and he had to get used to the stick he used to help him walk. He was also holding onto Sacred Bird's arm, which hindered her pace and made her lose her balance. The journey was slow and tiresome for Sacred Bird.

There were a few times they fell, and it was difficult for Eagle Crier to get up. It was during these times that Eagle Crier would stop trying to get up. He would tell her to go on without him. Sacred Bird would sit down by him and encourage him to go a little further. She did not want to leave him, and she did not want to travel alone.

After many days of travelling, Sacred Bird looked at the horizon. She could see the mountains under the clouds. This time she was not as excited as she would have been if her daughter and Eagle Crier's wife and child were with them. It seemed that her exhaustion had erased her emotions and she could not get excited about anything.

They did not make shelters at night, they just sat by the fires they made and slept sitting up or leaning against bushes. Not having a proper rest took a toll on their bodies, especially on Eagle Crier. His ankle was swollen so badly that he was in constant pain. They did not talk much as they travelled, only groans and grunts and the occasional cough.

It was one of the times that they fell and could not get up that Eagle Crier gave up. He sat where he fell and unwrapped his ankle. His ankle was swollen so big and it was almost black. There was nothing that Sacred Bird could do to help ease the pain.

With tears in his eyes, he turned to her and said, "You go on, I don't think I can make it. I am in great pain. I can't walk anymore."

Sacred Bird took his elbow and said, "you can't give up . . . you have to try. I thought about giving up, but I cannot lay down and die, we cannot lay down and die. You must try. When we get to that part of our journey, then we will greet death with dignity, right now we still have our life. We must be strong and keep going."

He had tears in his eyes. He patted Sacred Bird's hand and then started to wrap his ankle. She helped him up and with the first difficult step, they started slowly. This time Sacred Bird told him to lift himself up on the stick and she would hold him up as much as she could. She also suggested that they rest as often as they could.

They continued their journey. When Eagle Crier faltered, Sacred Bird did not have the strength to keep them both up. They would go down, but they always managed to get back up. The most difficult times were when they had to go down and up steep hills. After they tumbled down a hill, they decided that he would sit and move down the hill by using his arms and his one leg while Sacred Bird held his injured leg up to avoid jarring it. By the end of each day, they were so tired that they could only build a fire and eat a little of the porcupine.

One night as they sat, Eagle Crier asked if she knew how many days they had travelled alone. Sacred Bird told him she did not know. It was a subject she did not want to talk about, she did not want to remember the days when her daughter and his wife and baby died.

One day as they sat to rest, Sacred Bird noticed what looked like a valley. She nudged Eagle Crier and said, "Look, that looks like a river valley." She pointed to it, but Eagle Crier did not seem to be interested. She nudged him again, this time a little more sternly, "You must try . . . we must try to go a little further. We must try to get to the valley. I will be able to build a shelter and find food so that you can rest your ankle, then maybe the swelling will go down."

Eagle Crier reluctantly got up without saying a word. Sacred Bird could see the pain in his face. She could see how the pain and grief had aged him. His face had lines that were not there before, and he looked frail. Sacred Bird held him by his arm, and they started walking toward the valley.

It was nightfall by the time they reached the valley. Sacred Bird suggested they go down, and she would build a shelter and fire. They went down carefully. After she made the shelter and fire, she took out the last of the porcupine. It was not much but it would quiet their stomachs until she could secure food in the next day or so.

The next day, Sacred Bird told Eagle Crier to stay while she went to look for food. Eagle Crier did not object; he was content to stay off his ankle. Sacred Bird went out to the river first to see if there was a shallow part they could cross. She walked along the river and got to a bend that would be a good place to cross.

She headed back and scanned the surrounding trees to see if there was a porcupine she could kill for food. Her thoughts turned to the kind of food that had been sustaining her since she left the northern camp. She was no longer choosey about food, she needed to survive.

She headed back in the direction of the shelter and stopped to check on Eagle Crier. He was resting and she told him she would go again to search for food. She headed east. Along the way she picked up some rocks and a long stick to use as weapons. It was after midday when she headed back to the camp. She still did not get anything. The wind had changed direction and it looked like clouds were rolling in from the north. She feared it would snow and they would go hungry.

With a heavy heart, she headed back and thought how Eagle Crier would be disappointed. She scanned the trees, hoping to see a porcupine, and the ground for a rabbit, but there were no signs of any animals. It was late, almost dark when she headed back to the shelter.

Eagle Crier was sleeping, and the fire had died down. She added more wood to the fire and waited for Eagle Crier to wake up. Sacred Bird dozed off. When she awoke, she saw Eagle Crier wrapping his ankle. She sat up and asked him how his ankle was. He replied that it was still swollen and painful. He said he was cold and that wrapping his ankle prevented any sudden movement in his sleep and would help to avoid further injury.

Sacred Bird told him about not being able to get food. She told him she would go further west tomorrow and find food. Eagle Crier suggested she look for a place to cross the river. Sacred Bird told him that she found one just after the bend to the west of them.

With that information, Eagle Crier proceeded to make plans for the journey. Sacred Bird was glad to let him make plans, he knew this part of the land. Eagle Crier said he would look at the area they were at and determine the best way to go.

It was still dark when Sacred Bird woke up, but she could see the light from the rising sun through the trees. She was glad it did not snow. She decided not to add to the fire, they did not have food to warm up and they would have to cover it before they left. She decided she would look for a sturdier stick for Eagle Crier. She walked around the trees and found two, one was long and the other was a bit heavy. She took them both so he could choose the best one.

Eagle Crier was wrapping his ankle when she got back, and she gave him the two sticks to try them out. She said that if he could use both, she would still assist him and they could go a little faster. Eagle Crier stood up with Sacred Bird's help and took both sticks. After taking three steps, he told her that both were good.

They walked slowly toward the crossing that Sacred Bird had found the day before. There were a few obstacles they had to go around, but they made it to the crossing. Sacred

Bird suggested that Eagle Crier sit and rest while she went to test the crossing, just to make sure he could cross without falling into the river. She put on her extra pair of moccasins to walk in the water. She went across and found that there were a few big rocks in the water. He could avoid them by walking around them.

Sacred Bird returned and told Eagle Crier to switch his moccasins so that the left moccasin could stay dry. While he switched his moccasins, Sacred Bird took their robes and bags and brought them over to the other side of the river. Her feet were getting cold from crossing the river four times. She helped Eagle Crier walk over to the river's edge and they proceeded to walk slowly through the water. She told Eagle Crier that they had to go slow, that the rocks were slippery and he should carefully place each stick in between the rocks so they did not slip.

Although the river was not wide, it took them a long time to cross. She had to walk on his right and hold his elbow to help him keep his balance. He tried to keep his ankle out of the water, but it was impossible. Each time he moved one step, he would dip his foot in water. If he was in pain, he did not cry out or say it. Once they got to the other side, Sacred Bird led him to a tree trunk on the ground to sit on.

After a short rest and after they got their dry moccasins on, they decided to head west to find a place to get to the top of the hill. They rounded a bend and decided to rest; they were getting tired and hungry. Sacred Bird was too tired to look for small game. Eagle Crier suggested they go a little further before dark. They did not get very far when

Eagle Crier said he could smell smoke. Sacred Bird said she could smell it too.

They started again, and this time Eagle Crier told Sacred Bird to go ahead but to be careful and find out where the smoke was coming from. Sacred Bird walked as quickly as she could toward some trees and bushes. She found a little clearing in between the trees and bushes. She slowly peered around the trees and bushes to see a tepee among the trees. She noticed the faint smoke coming from the top of the tepee, that was what they were smelling. She did not see or hear anyone.

She did not know if she should be glad to find other people in this area. She did not go any further and headed back to Eagle Crier. She met Eagle Crier and told him about the tepee. Eagle Crier said he was glad and reassured Sacred Bird not to be afraid. He told her how some of the people camp in this area during this time. He told her they would get help and be home sooner, saying it was almost dark and they would have food and a place to rest.

Sacred Bird was not sure she should be happy. She knew she should be glad to get home sooner, but she could not trust any strangers. After much convincing, Sacred Bird agreed they should go to the tepee together.

They did not see or hear anyone as they approached the tepee. Eagle Crier tapped the entrance and called out to whoever might be inside. "Oki, I am Eagle Crier, and I am with Sacred Bird . . ." He paused before continuing, "Is anyone here?"

They stood outside the tepee for a few moments, but still there was no answer. Eagle Crier finally said, "There doesn't seem to be anyone here. Maybe we should just go in, they won't mind."

Eagle Crier cleared the sticks used to secure the entrance and entered. When he stopped abruptly, Sacred Bird almost knocked him down on the ground, but she was able to help him regain his balance. She looked down to see what made him stop. Seeing that there was nothing hindering his movement, she straightened and asked him why he stopped. Before she could finish her question, she followed his gaze to the other side of the tepee. They stood there staring at a man lying at the head of the tepee. He was dressed in full ceremonial dress. He looked like he was sleeping.

Eagle Crier stood trembling with fear. Sacred Bird started to tremble too. She held onto Eagle Crier to reassure herself that she was not alone. They both started to back out when Eagle Crier tripped and fell. Sacred Bird could not catch him, he lay there groaning from the pain of jarring his ankle.

Sacred Bird bent down to help Eagle Crier; she remembered the time her grandfather had died. The fact that Creator chose to call someone back to the Creator's sacred grounds was not to be feared if the person the Creator called had done all that was required.

She stepped forward. With her head held down, she spoke to the person, "Oki, I am Sacred Bird. Please have pity on us, we have come far. We overcame many obstacles and dangers. Please allow us to rest and we will be on our way . . . we will not disturb you . . . also please allow us to have some of your food . . . we will repay you later in the future."

She turned to Eagle Crier and told him that the person would not do anything to harm them. Eagle Crier did not argue, he was in pain and he was hungry. She spread the robe on the ground and helped him get comfortable. She searched for food that did not need to be cooked. She found food and portioned some for Eagle Crier and herself. They ate their fill, and the warmth of the tepee made them drowsy. They both fell asleep.

Sacred Bird awoke the next morning when she heard what sounded like a man clearing his throat. She sat up and looked around. She saw the man in ceremonial attire still lying in the same position, and then she remembered where they were.

She went to Eagle Crier and woke him up. She whispered that they did not want to overstay their welcome. He sat up and asked her if she had any water. She did not have any and said she would get some from the river.

Eagle Crier asked if they were going to eat before they left. Sacred Bird told him that she was sure they could eat a little, but it was not proper to take any food with them.

Sacred Bird tidied up before they left. Eagle Crier thanked the man for allowing them to rest and for the food. When they emerged from the tepee, the air was not as cold and there was a westerly wind. Eagle Crier instructed Sacred Bird to secure the tepee entrance with the sticks that he pushed out of the way when they first got there. Sacred Bird told Eagle Crier to start, and she would secure the tepee and catch up with him. She headed to the river to get water. She was not sure there would be water on the way.

She caught up with Eagle Crier. He had not gone far. He stopped to take a drink of the water. She asked if he thought about how he was going to climb the hill. The hill looked a little steep and she did not want him to injure his ankle more. He said he would have to sit and pull himself up backwards and would need her help. He also said he did not know how far he could travel.

It was past midday when they reached the top. As they surveyed the land, Eagle Crier said they would have to sit with their robes on as it was not wise to make a fire. They would try to get to a stream or river to make a fire.

They travelled south, their journey slow and uneventful. The snow on the ground was melting and they walked around snowdrifts that may hide a gully or an animal's burrow. They stopped to rest on dry ground on top of a hill. Eagle Crier was adjusting his ankle wrap and Sacred Bird was scanning the land ahead of them when she spotted a man on a horse. She did not say anything. She nudged Eagle Crier and pointed to the man on the horse. Eagle Crier looked and said the man looks and rides like the people from home. Sacred Bird still did not say anything and looked around to see if there were other riders.

The man approached them cautiously. Eagle Crier greeted him in Blackfoot and the greetings surprised him. The man prodded his horse and galloped toward them. He told Eagle Crier that he did not expect to find anyone out on the prairie. Sacred Bird did not recognize the man, but Eagle Crier seemed to know him.

Eagle Crier had forgotten the man's name. After introducing themselves, both men remembered each other.

Eagle Crier introduced Sacred Bird and told her that he and Akaomahkayii, Big Swan, knew each other as young men. After exchanging information as to why Eagle Crier and Sacred Bird came to be in this part of the land, Akaomahkayii offered his horse for them to ride. Akaomahkayii led the horse to his camp.

They arrived at Big Swan's camp just before it got dark. There were many camps. Curious people surrounded them as Big Swan led them to his tepee. Sacred Bird later learned that Big Swan was a minor chief. She was impressed with him. He had admirable qualities and his people were very fortunate to have him as their leader.

Their short stay as his guest was enjoyable, Eagle Crier and Sacred Bird briefly forgot the hardships they had endured. It was not hard to understand why Big Swan was a leader, his hospitality made them feel welcome. He urged his family to cater to his guests. His family was happy to attend to Eagle Crier and Sacred Bird's needs and make their stay comfortable.

Big Swan and his family prepared provisions for the travellers and they were very generous. They provided a horse for each to ride and food and water to last for the rest of the journey. After the farewells, Eagle Crier and Sacred Bird went on their way.

They headed in the direction of the high ridge. They knew this land and they were almost home. They did not put any undue stress on the horses, letting them travel at their pace. They rode in silence, each thinking of the loved ones they lost.

Sacred Bird would wipe the tears brought on by thinking of Sacred Feather Woman. Sacred Bird knew she would never forget her daughter or Eagle Crier's family. If only they had survived . . . Sacred Bird tried to think of other things, but the memory of Sacred Feather Woman was overwhelming.

She could see her smiling face and she could hear her sweet and gentle voice. She was a gentle and happy child. She had the ability to make Sacred Bird smile even in the worst of times. With tears streaming down her cheeks, Sacred Bird started thinking that she could not live without her daughter, and she wished that the events had turned out differently.

Still deep in her thoughts, Sacred Bird was startled when Eagle Crier broke the silence with a question. "Are those tears of happiness or tears of grief?"

Wiping the tears, she replied, "Both. I wish that Sacred Feather Woman, Walks With Porcupine Woman, and your baby had survived to see this land . . ."

"I know what you are going through. I too have thoughts about our loved ones and wish they were here. I wish that things had turned out better, but we have to accept events as the Creator has planned." Eagle Crier spoke with tears in his eyes as he tried not to break down. He steered his horse and patted her shoulder and said, "It is all right to remember them, we will not forget them. I know you have been strong, and I thank you for helping me. You have been the strong one. You made it possible for me to get here."

Sacred Bird did not talk anymore. They rode in silence. The horses picked up their pace as they climbed a hill. They were almost to the top of the hill when Sacred Bird looked back at the land they had just left.

The vast prairie was pretty that time of the winter. There were patches of white snow and prairie. The air was cooling, she could see it just above the ground, like a blue robe about to cover the ground. The setting sun peeked through the clouds just above the mountains. The clouds had the colours of fire. Sacred Bird stared at the scenery, trying to define each spectacular scene before it changed.

Eagle Crier called her and asked what she was staring at. She replied, "Nothing."

She turned and followed Eagle Crier. They reached the top of the hill and stood looking down on the land. The view took her breath away. For the first time in a long time, she could not find the words to describe the happiness she felt. She knew she would be seeing her loved ones soon.

Eagle Crier spoke first. "We are finally home, after so much suffering, pain, and sorrow. Sacred Bird, you are home! See that ridge over there?" he asked, pointing to a dark outline of a big hill, "That's where we will find our people."

Sacred Bird looked and replied, "Yes, I see it. I recognize it. It is hard to forget such a hill."

Sacred Bird knew that her journey would not be over when she reached her destination. She still had much to do to rebuild her life. Her family would be devastated to learn of Sacred Feather Woman's death.

CHAPTER 15

HOME

It was nightfall by the time Sacred Bird and Eagle Crier reached the first river they would have to cross before they could determine which direction they would go to reach the home camp. Eagle Crier got off his horse and suggested they camp for one last night.

He asked Sacred Bird to help him tie a rope to two trees so he could tie the horses to the rope. Sacred Bird was disappointed, but she knew they would have to wait for daylight to cross the river. She got off her horse and went to tie the rope to the two trees. Eagle Crier was still in pain and had taken one of the sticks to help him walk. Tying the horses for the night prevented them from wandering off.

Sacred Bird got a fire started. She found two short logs to sit on. She took the food from the pouches and waited for Eagle Crier to sit down. Eagle Crier hobbled over and sat down with great difficulty across from Sacred Bird. They ate the food that Akaomahkayii's family had provided. After the meal, Eagle Crier asked Sacred Bird if she knew where her home camp would be.

Sacred Bird replied, "I'm sure they would be camped by the river valley by the big ridge, I'm sure of it . . . I'm confused, it seems like it has been a long time since I was home, or they could be further east."

Eagle Crier nodded and said, "I agree, it has been a long time since we've been home. I'm not sure where my father and mother would be camped. They usually camp alternately with my father's and mother's clan. We will find them tomorrow."

Sacred Bird nodded as she packed the pouches. She secured the bags and went to hang them on a tree. She returned and asked Eagle Crier how his foot was.

He said, "It is still very sore and swollen. I don't think it's broken; I can move my toes a little bit. But it is painful. I still cannot stand on it." He unwrapped his ankle to relieve the pressure as Sacred Bird looked at it.

She said, "It is good we met your friend, or we might still be near the river valley we spent two nights at. It is good we have the two horses to ride, and we have food."

Eagle Crier agreed and said, "Yes, I was in so much pain hopping on one foot and holding onto you. Riding the horse is so much easier. I still have pain riding the horse but not as much."

They sat in silence, each with their own thoughts of loved ones. Sacred Bird thought about her children, her husband, and the grandparents. 'How will I fit in the family if I have been replaced by someone else?' This last thought brought a lump to her throat. She was determined not to cry, but the tears came anyway.

Eagle Crier noticed Sacred Bird wiping the tears and reassured her that everything would work out. "Don't worry, I am sure we will find your family and they will be glad you made it home. Let us get some rest and we will start out as soon as it is daylight. We will find a safe place to cross the river and head to the big ridge. We should be able to find a camp before nightfall."

Sacred Bird did not say anything, she got the robe and wrapped it over her shoulders. She hoped she could get some sleep. She thought about the nightly events that brought so much tragedy. She could not remember when they stopped. She felt angry at the source of those events. Could she have planned a different journey by herself? She could have persuaded Eagle Crier to take her daughter while she went on her own; after all, she was the target. She did not voice her thoughts, but they brought more tears.

Eagle Crier had already made himself comfortable on the other side of the campfire and was also deep in his own thoughts. Thoughts about his wife and baby. He knew he would be in mourning for a long time. He would have to find a way to go back and give his wife a proper burial once the weather permits. He would also have to consult with the elders before such a plan could be completed.

Sacred Bird woke early before the sun rose. She glanced at the grey clouds, hoping for a warmer day than the day before. The fire had died down. She wondered if she should build a fire, and after contemplating, she decided not to. She was eager to start the journey. She concluded that she would accept whatever was waiting for her at the home camp. She got up to get the food pouch from the tree and waited for Eagle Crier to wake up.

Sacred Bird sat patiently waiting for Eagle Crier to wake up. When he stirred, she was glad they would soon see loved ones. Eagle Crier sat up, rubbed his eyes, and smiled at Sacred Bird. He said, "You look like you cannot wait to start the final day of the journey."

Sacred Bird said, "I am looking forward to seeing my loved ones and whatever awaits me. What about you? Are you glad we are nearing the end of the journey?"

Eagle Crier replied, "I am glad, maybe I can get proper treatment for my ankle, and I can walk without this stick. I know the elders will be able to help me. Hopefully I have not damaged my ankle too much."

Sacred Bird replied, "That is true. I don't think it's damaged too much. Let us eat before we go."

After they finished eating, Sacred Bird told Eagle Crier that she would get the horses. Eagle Crier got on the horse with Sacred Bird's help. They walked the horses along the shore of the river to find a place to cross. They crossed the river at a spot where they could see the bottom without any sheets of ice.

They rode in silence for a while before Eagle Crier spoke. He turned to Sacred Bird and asked her, "Have you heard any more noises in the last few nights? I was wondering, you seem to be a light sleeper, you're always up before I wake up."

Sacred Bird answered, "No, I was thinking about them last night and I could not remember when I last heard them."

Eagle Crier said, "I am quite sure the last time was four nights before we lost Walks With Porcupine Woman. I was thinking about them last night too, and I am quite sure I was going to be next. Injuring my ankle was a misfire. I think, when we get to your home camp, we will have to seek the advice of the elders and the medicine man."

Sacred Bird agreed and said, "I had not thought of seeking advice. I was too consumed with the fact that I will see loved ones, especially my children. Yes, I agree we will let them know as soon as we get to the home camp, and they can help us. I think I am the one they need to cleanse. The elders and the medicine man will tell us what to do."

They reached the next river before midday. The cold westerly wind was penetrating through their clothing. They stopped so that Sacred Bird could help Eagle Crier put the robe over his shoulders to keep warm. She also put her robe over her shoulders to keep warm. They proceeded to look for a place to cross the river.

Once they crossed the river, they had to go through trees and thick bushes to reach the top of the hill. The trees and thick bushes brought painful memories of that spring day. She tried not to shed any tears, there would be plenty of time to mourn with family. When they got to the top of the hill, Eagle Crier suggested they stop and rest. He told Sacred Bird he needed to adjust the wrapping on his ankle. Sacred Bird helped him get off his horse so he could sit on the ground to adjust the wrapping.

Sacred Bird decided that was a good time to eat. There were a few snow patches, but the ground was mostly bare of snow. The horses grazed on the prairie grass as Eagle Crier and Sacred Bird sat on the grass to eat their meal. After they ate, Sacred Bird helped Eagle Crier get back on the horse and they headed toward the big ridge. Sacred Bird scanned the horizon and could not see any camps or animals.

They headed east along the top of the hill, the horses walking briskly on the prairie grass. Eagle Crier scanned the land by the big ridge. Seeming to spot something, he stopped his horse to take a better look. He called Sacred Bird, who had gotten further ahead, "Sacred Bird, those animals I'm seeing over by the ridge . . ." he began, pointing to them, "Are those horses?"

Sacred Bird turned her horse around and stopped by Eagle Crier, looking in the direction he was pointing. She looked and said, "I don't think so, those look like deer, some of them are starting to run as if to run away from something."

Eagle Crier said, "Yes, you are right, they are all starting to run except for one, they are deer. I was hoping they were horses. Once we go past that little coulee, there might be a camp."

They resumed their journey, each scanning the different directions to see any sign of the people that usually camp close to the big ridge. The wind from the west was a little stronger, it seemed to push them as they headed east. They got through two coulees with thick bushes. Sacred Bird had to lead so that Eagle Crier would not get his ankle caught in the bushes and injure it more. In some places the bushes hid a small dirt cliff, but the horses would see it and veer off.

They rested after the second coulee, and it was well past midday. Eagle Crier was a little concerned that they had not encountered anyone since they crossed the two rivers.

Sacred Bird agreed and asked, "What season is it? Which moon is it? It's been so long since we left the northern camp, I have lost track."

Eagle Crier said, "You are right, it has been a long journey, I have lost track . . . I am not sure . . . it cannot be the Eagle Moon. Let's keep going before it gets dark."

They headed toward a small hill. This time the horses walked a little faster, as if sensing an urgency to get to their destination. Sacred Bird and Eagle Crier did not hold back the horses, they allowed them to walk fast. They also wanted to reach their destination as soon as possible. They reached the top of the small hill and stopped to survey the land ahead of them.

Eagle Crier said, "It's hard to see any smoke with the wind blowing so hard, but we should keep heading in this direction, maybe we will come upon a camp."

They started again. It was getting dark. They were down a little hill when they heard dogs barking very faintly. They both looked at each other and urged their horses to walk faster, each expecting to see a camp on the other side of the hill. Sacred Bird could not wait to reach the top of the hill ahead of them and she could almost see the camp, which was not in view yet.

At the top of the hill, they could see the camp. There were many tepees. They were still far from the camp, but they could see movement. They looked at each other, each smiling with excitement to see their people, especially loved ones. They did not have to say anything, they both knew they were home!

Eagle Crier told Sacred Bird she could go faster if she wanted, but Sacred Bird told him they would both get to the camp at the same time. As they neared the camp, the dogs seemed to run and greet them. The dogs' barking brought more people out to see what the dogs were barking at.

Eagle Crier waved to let the people know they were approaching peacefully. Some of the young men came out to meet and greet them. Sacred Bird did not recognize any of them, but they understood Eagle Crier's greeting. Two young men took the horses and led them toward the camp.

The people of the camp surrounded them, and some assisted Eagle Crier. After the introductions, they were led to the tepee of one of the leaders. The leader introduced himself as Iikoh'tsi moo nissi (Yellow Otter). He turned to Sacred Bird and told her that he was a close relative, having the same grandparents as her father.

Sacred Bird told him that she remembered him. She and Eagle Crier spoke with Yellow Otter and the Elders into the night after they were served a very good and filling meal. Some of the information shared that night brought tears and laughter. Yellow Otter and his wife made their guests feel welcome. Yellow Otter told Sacred Bird that he would accompany her to her home camp the next day.

He reassured her that she would see loved ones tomorrow and that she must rest tonight. A very kind woman, Dark Eyed Woman, a relative of Yellow Otter's wife, led Sacred Bird to her tepee to rest for the night. Sacred Bird would finally have a good night's rest in a warm bed and not out in the open.

After a restless night, Sacred Bird woke to the noises of the dogs and children outside the tepee. She looked around, she was the only one in the tepee, the other women were not there. She got up and wondered if Yellow Otter was waiting for her to get up, so she hurried and got ready.

She went outside and looked around to see if the people were waiting for her. Seeing no one with horses, she walked over to Yellow Otter's tepee. She stood for a moment outside, wondering if that was the tepee, and then she heard Yellow Otter call her to tell her to enter. She entered. The warmth and aroma of food greeted her as well as the greetings from Yellow Otter and his wife.

Everyone was seated in the tepee, and she sat down by the entrance as a young lady served her. She sat and ate and listened to the conversation of the people. After she finished, Yellow Otter told her the young men were preparing the horses for the ride to her home camp. Eagle Crier was seated next to Yellow Otter. He told her he would not be travelling with her because he needed to be off his ankle.

Sacred Bird told him, "That's all right, you need to take care of your foot so that it can heal. I am grateful for your help and for your company. I will remember you in my prayers."

Eagle Crier said, "I am the one that is grateful. You helped me get here, but I am glad you will be seeing your loved ones today. I have told Yellow Otter about our journey. He and the Elders will help me with what needs to be done and he will help me find my parents."

With that, Yellow Otter got up and said, "The young men are ready with the horses, we will leave now."

Sacred Bird got up and went outside to the waiting men and horses. Ten young men and Yellow Otter would accompany Sacred Bird to her home camp. They headed east toward a hill. They rode in silence for most of the way. The morning was cool and there was no wind; it made the ride pleasant. Sacred Bird was content to ride in silence.

Yellow Otter did not say too much, he was a man with few words. He spoke when he had to and usually to the young men. They reached the hill before midday. As they got to the top of the hill, Sacred Bird recognized this land. She and her husband had travelled through here countless times.

She wondered what awaited her, she was excited to see her sons and her husband. She could not define the emotions she was feeling. She also had regrets about the death of Sacred Feather Woman. Her feeling of excitement always turned to sorrow whenever she thought about Sacred Feather Woman.

Yellow Otter stopped at the last hill, pointed north to what looked like tepees, and told Sacred Bird, "See those tepees? That is where your family is. They will be glad to see you after how many winters?" He asked, turning to Sacred Bird.

Sacred Bird replied, "It has been a long time, over two winters."

Yellow Otter said, "Yes, that is a long time. We should be there soon."

They walked the horses down the steep slope, avoiding rocks jutting out from the ground. The horses seemed to know where to step as they got down the hill and proceeded to go up the next hill. Sacred Bird did not have any problems riding the horses through the hills, she was becoming an experienced rider.

When they got through the hills, the rest of the way was easy riding, mostly prairie and few bushes. As they neared the camp, Sacred Bird felt excitement. She looked forward to seeing her family. She did her best to contain her excitement and tried to remain calm, but it was a struggle to maintain her composure.

A few people came to greet them, some shouting to their families that Yellow Otter had come, not really noticing Sacred Bird. Once they got into the camp, some recognized Sacred Bird and the noise of excitement increased. Sacred Bird was caught off guard as the people clambered to get near her.

They got off the horses. The young men with Yellow Otter took the horses and led them away to tie them to the trees. Everyone was talking all at once and crowding around them, it was hard for Sacred Bird to see her immediate family. As she was looking around, she felt someone touch her shoulder and as she turned to look, her husband was behind her. She hesitated for a few moments. Without any words, he gave her a big hug. That was a pleasant surprise, she had not anticipated a welcome like that.

Yellow Otter and Little Owl, an Elder, came and led them to a tepee. Sacred Bird was overwhelmed with excitement, she did not know how she could tell the story of her journey. Yellow Otter reassured her that he would help her since Eagle Crier had told him of the journey from the northern camp. Sacred Bird felt relieved, but she still needed to see her sons.

Just then, two boys came and gave her a big hug. She was surprised at their height; how they had grown, and so tall! Tears streaming down her cheeks, she hugged them and told them how she missed them. Her younger son was the first to ask about Sacred Feather Woman. Sacred Bird told him that she would tell them as soon as they got into the tepee, because it was a long story.

As soon as everyone was seated in the tepee, Yellow Otter and the Elders welcomed Sacred Bird back into the clan. They also had the Medicine Man present to help with a small ceremony to help Sacred Bird feel safe. After the short ceremony, Sacred Bird told them what she went through when she and Sacred Feather Woman got taken. It was painful for her to recount the events of that day, but she managed to finish the story.

Yellow Otter told the story of the journey home. Sacred Bird was glad she did not have to tell the story, it was a painful experience. She knew she would have to tell the story later during her lifetime, but for now she was thankful that Eagle Crier had told the story to Yellow Otter. It was much better that Yellow Otter told the story, he could tell it without getting emotional and without tears.

GLOSSARY

Blackfoot words:

Ah saa . . . . What is it? (a reply)

AKainiwa . . . . . . Many Chiefs Tribe

Akaomahkayii . . . . Big Swan

Na'aa. . . . . Mother

Naatoyipi'kssi . . . . Sacred Bird

Oki . . . . greeting, hello.

Iikoh'tsi moo nissi . . . . . .Yellow Otter

Cree:

Ko'kom . . . . Grandmother

ABOUT THE AUTHOR

Pearl Long Time Squirrel is herself a member of the Blood Reserve and a descendant of Sacred Bird. Her cousin's encouragement inspired Pearl to write the story of Sacred Bird. The woman's inspiring story of survival, determination, and overcoming has been passed down through the generations. By putting the story of Sacred Bird on paper, Pearl hopes to record and preserve the stories of heroes and heroines she heard throughout her life to ensure this story, among others, is not lost.

Pearl Long Time Squirrel lives on the Blood Reserve in southern Alberta with her son, grandson, and Basset Hound Molly. Outside of writing, she enjoys sewing, beading, crocheting, writing poems, and gardening.

Printed in Canada